MW01444654

A ROGUE COWBOY'S KISS

A HART RANCH BILLIONAIRE'S NOVEL

STEPHANIE ROWE

For all the women out there who need a little reminder that you're awesome, you matter, and you never, EVER need to apologize for who you are, what you want, or how you feel. Because you're amazing, exactly as you are.

COPYRIGHT

ACKNOWLEDGMENTS

Special thanks to my beta readers. You guys are the best!

There are so many to thank by name, more than I could count, but here are those who I want to called out specially for all they did to help this book come to life: Alyssa Bird, Anette Taylor, Ashlee Murphy, Brenda Wasnock, Bridget Koan, Britannia Hill, Carolena Emer, Cindy Abbott, Deb Julienne, Denise Fluhr, Diana Kassman, Dottie Jones, Elizabeth Barnes, Heidi Hoffman, Helen Loyal, Jackie Moore Kranz, Jeanne Stone, Jeanie Jackson, Jessica Hayden, Jodi Bobbett, Jodi Moore, Judi Pflughoeft, Kasey Richardson, Linda Rogers, Linda Watson, Nichole Reed, Regina Thomas, Summer Steelman, Suzanne Mayer, Shell Bryce, Susan Parker, and Trish Douglas. Special thanks to my family, who I love with every fiber of my heart and soul. And to AER, who is my world. Love you so much, baby girl! I am so proud of you! You're going to rock this world! And to Joe, who keeps me believing myself. I love you all!

PRAISE FOR STEPHANIE ROWE

"The Harts will definitely capture your heart. They are healing, overprotective, badasses that you want in your circle." Five-star Goodreads Review (Jill T)

"Phew. There were some big, big feels in this book. The emotions were really the driving force in this story so buckle up. You get all the swoony swoons while also having your heartstrings pulled by all the intense emotions…The characters are so three dimensional they could almost walk off the page." Five-star Goodreads Review (Tammy M)

"Let me tell you why I enjoy Stephanie Rowe's books. They are full of heart. You literally fall in love with the characters. As a reader you are drawn into the story, invested in the outcome. Stephanie Rowe has a way of grabbing your attention from page one and before you know it hours have passed and the book is finished." Five-star Goodreads Review (KReid09)

"Stephanie is a master at weaving a great romcom filled with adventure, mishaps, laughter, intrigue, and love. This story made me feel all the feels and I look forward to the series as it unfolds." ~5-star Goodreads Review (Heidi)

"I love these emotionally charged stories. They hit you right in the heart." Five-star Goodreads Review (April M)

"I love how Stephanie Rowe builds a story. First, you become so captivated and involved with the characters, that you become their first row cheering section. Then she creates a story that sucks you in from the beginning and with the twists and turns that occur, you can't put the book down until it's finished…I love this more light-hearted, humorous, yet emotional spin-off from the Hart family series. There's lots of excitement, intrigue, emotions, and humor; all classic elements of a Stephanie Rowe story that combine for a five-star read." ~5-star Goodreads Review (Elizabeth)

"Stephanie Rowe hit another one out of the park!" 5-star Goodreads Review (Denise P)

"Stephanie Rowe has a way of grabbing your attention from page one and before you know it hours have passed and the book is finished." ~5-star Goodreads Review (KReid09)

"I cannot ever say enough about the genius of Stephanie Rowe. I've loved all her books across all the genres she writes… This book has it all. Laughs, cries, finger-biting. Everything. Lovers of mysteries, cozy mysteries, romance and books in general will love reading this installment. I can't recommend it highly enough. Can I make it 5+ stars? 6? 100? I would if I could." 5-star Goodreads Review (Jeanne S.)

"This one grabbed me from the first sentence and took me along for a hilarious and twisty ride. This was a stay up too late because I could not put it down kind of book." 5-star Goodreads Review (Tammy M.)

"This book is pure genius. Hilariously funny all the way through and with a fantastic storyline too." 5-star Goodreads Review (Nikki P)

"OMG!!! The best yet!! Stephanie has outdone herself! I am in love with this book. I was on an emotional roller coaster. I just love the banter, love and laughter." ~5-star Goodreads Review (Cindy A)

"I laughed, I cried, I had to stop and compose myself. But I had a hard time putting it down." 5-star Goodreads Review (Laura C.)

"Masterful... tugged at my heart." 5-star Goodreads Review (Elizabeth)

"I fell head over heels for Leila and Dash! Their story made me laugh, cry, and swoon!" 5 stars, Jessie's Reading Corner

"Exquisitely beautiful!! All the feels. This is a do not pass up book. Perfectly written :)." 5-star Goodreads Review (Jann)

ONE

FALCON PAUSED, hands on his thighs, gasping for air. The torrential rain was icy cold, barely above freezing, and the wind was knifing through him. He was cold all the way to his gut, but it didn't matter. He'd been this cold many times. He felt like he lived in this level of cold, and it had never stopped him before.

He would never stop.

Never stop hiding, and never stop hunting.

He'd been so close a dozen times, and the ghost had always slipped through his fingers.

But today...today felt different.

Something was humming inside Falcon, an energy that felt intoxicating and poisonous at the same time.

He looked up at the trail ahead of him. He'd been climbing for hours, following the faint trail of clues he'd been uncovering for almost twenty years.

He saw, up ahead, a glint, and he stiffened.

He pulled out his binoculars and saw there was a hut up ahead. Small. Wooden. Blue trim.

Son of a bitch.

It was really there. But was it the hut he'd been looking for?

He paused to consult his spirit guides, to hear the truth inside him that he'd learned to listen to. In the dark places he'd spent much of his life, he'd learned to find relief in places that he never would have expected, like tapping into the higher truth and guidance that didn't judge him for being the man he was. *Is this the place?* he asked.

Yes.

The answer was clear and unequivocal. His guides didn't give him much, but most of the time, when it really mattered, he could get a sense of yes and no if he asked the right question.

There had been no doubt about the answer they gave him this time.

This was it. This time, it would end.

He shoved his binoculars in his pocket and pulled out his gun, stepping off the trail into the wet underbrush and moving out of sight.

Years of living on the edge of humanity had taught him to blend into the vegetation, as he moved silently and swiftly up the mountain, closing in on the cabin that he hoped like hell held the man who had consumed him since he was ten.

The Harts, his found family, had told him so many times to give up, to build a home on their Oregon ranch, to let himself live.

He wanted to. Every damned night, he dreamed of that ranch, of waking up in a bed, in a home. Of walking out the front door and being able to breathe. To be with the horses. To have dinner with people he cared about every night, not just when he skated into town on the back of a shadow.

He dreamed of *her*. Every damned night.

But he couldn't choose that for himself. He couldn't walk away from this life. This was all that mattered to him.

2

The sun was setting, casting the stormy mountain into long shadows as he forced his exhausted body to forge ahead.

He reached the clearing beside the hut and crouched, watching, waiting. Was he home? Was this *monster* he'd been playing cat and mouse with for so long there? Waiting for Falcon? Was this a trap that would end Falcon? Or the prize that would finally set him free?

Falcon reached out with his mind, and he could feel the undercurrent of dense energy surrounding the house. He didn't know the energy signature of the man he'd been hunting, but this felt like what he would have imagined it to be.

Falcon waited in the underbrush for several hours, watching for any sign that the hut was occupied.

There was no movement. Not even a whisper.

So Falcon waited some more, patient. Willing to wait for the end of this quest that had been his life for two decades.

It was after three in the morning when Falcon finally eased from the bushes, sliding through the shadows hiding from the moon, working his way to the hut.

He paused outside the door, listening, his senses attuned to the night for a breath that was out of place, a leaf that shouldn't be moving, an alert from the animals who made this mountain their home…

But there was nothing.

So Falcon tried the door.

Locked.

He quickly remedied that, and then eased the door open.

He waited for someone to shoot him or stab him, but no one moved.

After one more check behind him to make sure he wasn't walking into a trap, he leaned around the corner, shining his penlight, gun ready, scanning the interior.

There was a man on the floor, sprawled face down.

Falcon studied the man for a long moment, but his face was turned away. He didn't know if it was the man he'd come for. But his heart started racing, and he felt like it was. Like it was *him*.

But Falcon had to be sure before he pulled the trigger. Had to be sure he wasn't going to perpetuate the legacy of his father by killing an innocent.

He stepped into the room, fully alert to every sound, scent, and whisper of information on the wind, but he could sense no threat.

His boots silent on the wooden floor, Falcon approached the inert figure. He saw a photo in one of the man's hands…a photo of Falcon less than a year ago, with Bella Hart, the sister of the men he considered his brothers, none of whom were related by blood. Only by heart.

His gut congealed at the sight of Bella's face. *Fuck.* He'd stayed away from her to keep her safe, and this monster had known all along that she was his kryptonite?

Sudden rage burst through him. With a roar of fury, of twenty years of pent-up rage, Falcon leapt across the floor, grabbed the man by his shoulder, and hauled him to the side, rolling him over so he could see his face.

Falcon's gut contracted when he saw the face, the face of his memories, the face that had taunted him, hurt him, scared him, and haunted his every moment for so long. The face of the man who had stolen everything from Falcon.

It was *him*.

But his glazed, unfocused eyes and the emptiness of the air around him told Falcon that someone had beat him to it.

He was dead, and Falcon hadn't been the one to pull the trigger.

It was *over*.

After twenty years…it was over.

Falcon's legs gave out and he went down to his knees, suddenly too weak to stand. He bowed his head, fighting to control the emotions running through him, the images flashing through his mind. He fought off the memories, fought off the past, fought off both the relief and disappointment that he hadn't been the one to end it.

It took only a second, maybe two, before Falcon raised his head. Whoever had killed him might still be around. There was no time to process. He had to get out.

He shoved the man away from him, grabbed the photo of Bella, and then staggered to his feet. He did a quick search of the cabin, tension wrapping tighter and tighter as he found more pictures of himself, of Bella, of the Harts, and their ranch in Oregon. This monster had known so much about him, toying with him for so long. Except for the initial photo of himself and Bella, Falcon took every last bit of evidence of the Harts and himself and shoved it into the wood stove. He lit it, and stood there, watching until the pile that represented his heart was consumed by flames.

He stood, staring into that fire, into the orange flames, fully focused on what he was doing. On making sure the people he loved were safe.

Once the pictures were gone, he closed the wood stove, strode to the door, and walked out, not turning around, not looking back, walking away from the past that had trapped him for so long.

He made it halfway down the mountain before he dropped to his knees and bent over, his knees sinking into the mud, his chest burning with pain, his mind spinning as his brain fought to grasp the truth.

The purpose he'd had since he was ten was gone.

The man he'd had to be since he was ten was no longer needed.

The life he'd endured for so long had no purpose anymore.

Who he was…was over.

What was left for him? Who the hell was he now?

He looked down at the photo in his hand, at the woman he'd known since he was twenty and she was sixteen. *Bella.*

5

He closed his eyes, letting the rain wash down his cheeks, breathing in the cold, cold water as it seemed to cleanse a lifetime of filth from his skin.

Bella.

Did he dare?

He looked down at his knees, buried in the mud. At his pants, wet, torn, dirty. He touched his face, the rough beard he never seemed to care enough about to keep trimmed.

He'd been on the run for so long, he felt like a wild animal.

He *was* a wild animal, in truth.

But there was one place on this earth where he didn't have to be civilized, pretend he was okay, or talk to people who didn't understand the darkness that still clung to him, and always would.

That place was the Hart Ranch in Oregon, home of the nine Hart siblings, the place the Harts had been offering him for so long.

Finally, he could go there.

To the men who were his family, even though he had never let them in.

To Bella, who right now, would be in her kitchen on the dude ranch part of the Hart ranch, working her magic, whipping up fantastic grub for her guests. He thought of her sassy smile, her favorite pink cowboy hat, and her pink camo pants that she loved to wear when she was four-wheeling around the ranch.

He'd never made a move on her.

Not once.

Not ever.

Not even when she was sixteen and she'd begged him for a kiss.

Because he'd known there was a monster following him, and he'd never risk any of the Harts, especially not Bella.

But now...he took a breath. The monster was dead.

Falcon was damaged goods. Dirty. Scarred.

He knew that.

But he also knew the Harts didn't care about that, because they all carried their own stories.

Was he too scarred for Bella?

Probably.

He paused to ask his guides. *Should I walk away from Bella?*

He waited, but there was only silence. Was it because the answer was to walk away, and he didn't want to hear it? Or because his guides already knew he'd made up his mind?

Maybe he wasn't enough for her.

Maybe he was.

But it was time to find out.

After all these years, it was time to find out.

He dragged himself to his feet and started hiking down the mountain again…walking faster. And faster.

Until he was in a dead-on sprint, and it still wasn't fast enough.

TWO

BELLA TOOK A BREATH, surprised by how nervous she was.

She'd made thousands of dinners for family, friends, and all the dude ranch guests. She knew what she was doing when it came to food.

But this was different.

"You look terrified."

Bella looked over at her sister Meg Hart, who had come to Boston for the evening to help her. Meg looked gorgeous in a calf-length emerald silk dress that made her brown skin radiate with beauty.

"I am kind of terrified," Bella admitted.

"Why? You cook all the time."

"I know. I just…"

Meg smiled. "You don't want to mess this up."

Bella took a breath and nodded. "Piper and Kitty did me a huge favor by letting me cater this wedding. And I don't want to blow it." Piper Townsend, a wedding planner, and Kitty Jones, a former popstar now in her sixties, were the owners of a brand-new boutique event-planning firm called ToJo Events. They'd formed ToJo to focus on weddings, but a cancelled wedding and a girl power moment had inspired a surge of parties by women, for women, celebrating women.

After growing up surrounded by brothers, Bella had fallen madly in love with the female friendship and support that Piper, Maddie, and the others had so generously included her and Meg in.

Meg raised her brows. "You do know you're a billionaire, right? You don't need this job."

"But I do need it." Bella watched Piper and Kitty hurry through the ballroom, making last minute adjustments on the tables. Their friend, Maddie Vale, who was now Bella's sister-in-law, and how Bella had met Piper, was making final touches on the flowers. Maddie's two other friends, Tori and Keira, were also there, all of them racing around and having fun, cheering each other on as they worked to have it ready by the time the two brides arrived. "Not for money. For my soul."

Meg nodded slowly. "I get it. These women have the most amazing friendship, and they've welcomed us in. It feels pretty special."

"I know." Bella tucked her arm through Meg's. "I love our brothers and the ranch, but I feel like I've been trapped there for so long. Coming to Boston, getting to know these women, and cooking for this happy event…it just feels amazing."

Meg cocked her brow. "You want to stay, don't you?"

Bella shrugged. "I just got here two days ago." She'd stayed in Oregon for the whole season of the dude ranch, but the minute their last guest had left, she'd packed her bags and hopped on one of their jets. She'd been counting the days until she could come, and it had been everything she'd wanted. Everything she'd hoped for. "I feel like I'm free for the first time in my life."

Meg glanced over at her. "You know you're not actually free, right? You know that he's still out there somewhere.

He'll find you if you start appearing on social media for this company."

"I know." Bella pressed her lips together for a minute. "Watching Maddie be brave made me feel like a wimp for hiding for so long. I can do it." She patted her gun that was hidden under her left arm. "I got a license to carry concealed in Massachusetts, and I could kill at least some men with my bare hands."

"I know, but…" Meg sighed. "I just love you. I'll miss you at the ranch. I don't want you to move out here, even as much as I want you to have the life you want."

Bella's throat tightened. "I'm not going anywhere," she said finally. "It's just an adventure for a few weeks. A working vacation." But the thought of going back to the ranch made her throat constrict.

She loved the ranch. She loved her brothers and Meg. But ever since she'd met Maddie a few months ago, living this amazing life in Boston, something inside Bella had come alive and refused to go back to sleep.

What did she want? She didn't know.

But she knew she wasn't going to find it on the Hart Ranch, with cowboys, horses, a shared past of trauma, homelessness, and her specialty, pulled-pork sandwiches.

Kitty Jones, the popstar turned country-club-maven, record exec, and the sassiest woman Bella had ever met, jogged up, moving with an energy that made it seem like her concerts would have been amazing. Kitty might have kids in their thirties, but she had enough zest and zeal to put any thirty-something to shame. "The wedding ceremony's over. Everyone's on the way. ETA fifteen minutes. You good?"

Energy shot through Bella. "My team's ready." Bella had hired a local catering staff, using her money and connections to put together a team she could count on, even though they'd been together for only two days.

Kitty winked at her. "You look terrified. Bella, today isn't about perfection. It's about the power of women, it's about love, and all sorts of fun stuff. We deliver full-on girl power, not sterile perfection. So, go be real, be delicious, and just let your amazing talents out into the world. Got it?"

Bella let out a breath. How much did she love this woman? Kitty reminded her so much of Bella's mom, back before she'd been sucked into the world of drugs and addiction when Bella was fourteen. "Thanks, Kitty. I'll try to relax."

"Don't relax! Energize!" Kitty pointed at Meg. "You. I need help moving tables. Bring that gorgeous emerald dress with you and come help."

Meg shot a look at Bella as she followed Kitty. "I'll be back in a sec."

"No worries. I got this." Bella took a moment to breathe in the beautiful Cape Cod vista overlooking the ocean that surged with energy. God, she wanted to be a part of this world so much, to feel the purpose that Kitty and Piper did. To feel like she mattered.

To feel seen.

To feel like a woman who was badass, free, and beautiful.

Not like a woman who was scared, hid in her beautiful ranch, and smelled like horses and garlic every night when she walked in the door.

Kitty looked over at Bella and gestured impatiently, waving her out of the room.

"Right. I'm going!" Bella turned away and headed toward the kitchen. She shook the nervousness out of her shoulders, and then pushed open the door to the kitchen. "Fifteen minutes," she called out. "Let's go!"

THREE

DUST ROSE UP from his truck tires as Falcon pulled up in front of Brody Hart's house. Brody was the oldest Hart, the one who had taken care of all the Hart homeless truants when they were little, the reason they had all survived their teenage years.

Brody was also the one Falcon felt closest to, because it was Brody who reiterated the invite to move to the ranch every single week.

It would be Brody he would tell first.

Plus...he felt like he owed him the truth.

The front door opened as Falcon got out of his pickup.

Brody walked out, wearing jeans, cowboy boots, a Tatum Crosby concert tee shirt, and a dark brown cowboy hat. He looked every bit a cowboy, nothing like a billionaire tech genius who had once lived under a bridge.

"Falcon," Brody said, jogging down the stairs to greet him. "You look like you've been in hell for the last month. You okay?"

Falcon nodded. He was tired. He was hungry. He was dirty. He'd come straight here from the mountain, which meant it had been almost forty-eight hours since he'd slept. "He's dead."

Brody stopped. "Did you kill him?"

"No. He was dead when I got there. New dead. Didn't see who did it, but yeah, dead. There were pictures of the family there. Ranch, too. He knew about all of you. I burned all the shit. But maybe the guy who killed him knows about you guys. Maybe—"

"Shut up." Brody walked up to him and threw his arms around him. "Shut the fuck up, Falcon. Breathe."

Falcon closed his eyes as the man he considered his brother hugged him. He hadn't stopped in so long. Hadn't stood still in so long. Hadn't felt his soul rest in so long. But standing there in that driveway, he felt something inside him shift. Not rest. But shift.

He didn't hug Brody back, because he didn't know how, but he stood there, and didn't step away.

Brody eventually stepped back. "We will absolutely take precautions in case anyone decides to show up, but I doubt they will. It was between you and him, and whoever killed him probably had their own beef."

Falcon nodded again. Emotions coagulated around him again, and suddenly, he didn't want to talk about it.

He didn't want to tell Brody he was moving to the ranch.

Right now, he just wanted to see Bella. She was the only one who ever made him feel like there wasn't a coating of dirt on his soul. "Bella over at the restaurant? Thought I'd go see if she needs help."

Brody's brows went up, and he gave Falcon a look. "She's in Boston."

"Boston?" Falcon was suddenly tired. So fucking tired. "When's she coming back?"

Brody shrugged. "I don't know. She went there to help out with Maddie and Kitty's business. I think she's planning to stay a while." He sighed. "She's been restless out here, Falcon. I've been watching it, and I know she's gotta go. But I don't like it."

Falcon took a step back. "She's *staying* in Boston?"

"Again, I don't know." Brody frowned. "You all right?"

Bella. In Boston.

All Falcon wanted was to stop running and park his ass on this ranch. Be with the horses. With the people who let him be. With the woman he'd loved for a million fucking years. "She's staying in Boston?" he asked again.

Brody narrowed his eyes. "What's going on with you? When was the last time you slept?"

"A couple days." Falcon strode away, clasping his hands on his head as he stared across the vast lands of the Hart enclave. There were horses grazing. A state-of-the-art barn. And land that stretched into the horizon, a place where there was silence and peace, where noise didn't ever enter, unless a man asked for it.

The place where Bella had made her home.

It had never occurred to Falcon that he wouldn't be able to come back here, settle in, and find Bella. It had just never crossed his mind. This oasis had always been the humanity that had kept him from losing himself to the darkness all this time.

And she was gone?

"Falcon." Brody's voice was low. "You know the rules."

Falcon knew the rule Brody was talking about. When they were homeless teenagers living under the bridge, Brody had instituted a rule that they never hid secrets from each other. They never suffered alone. They always shared their truth, no matter what. It had been that rule that had created the bond that had held them all together, because it made each of them realize they weren't alone, they weren't going to be judged, and there might not be an answer, but there was comfort.

14

Falcon had never taken the last name of Hart like the other nine, and he'd kept his distance on some levels, but that didn't mean he wasn't part of their inner circle. It also didn't mean the rules didn't apply, at least when it came to Brody.

So he answered the question. "I love Bella."

There was silence for a long moment, and Falcon hardened himself. He knew what a fuck-up he was. Did Bella deserve more than him? Yeah. And Brody would tell him that.

"What else?"

Falcon turned to look at Brody, who was still staring across the horizon. "I said I love Bella. Not as a sister."

"You've loved her since the first moment you met her," Brody said, turning to look at him. "I wondered how long it would take for you to admit it to yourself."

Falcon was stunned by Brody's answer. "You knew?"

"Yeah."

"Does she?"

"Not that I know of." Brody paused. "She doesn't want any man to fall in love with her, you know. She doesn't trust love. Romance. Relationships."

Falcon nodded. "I know." He hadn't worried that Bella would be taken, because he knew how completely she shut out love. But he hadn't expected her to move away.

"So, what else is going on?"

Falcon smiled then, relief easing the ache in his gut. "I had this plan to move back here, build a house, see if I could win Bella's heart, and then never leave the ranch again."

Brody laughed softly. "Spoken like a man who has been outside the edges of functioning society for a very long time."

Falcon rubbed the back of his neck, exhaustion beginning to weigh him down. "Yeah, well…yeah."

They were both quiet for a moment, then Falcon grinned. "You're not going to tell me to stay away from her, are you?"

"Nope." Brody raised his brows. "She's perfectly capable of kicking your ass to the curb if she feels like it. Bella doesn't need my protection anymore. I'm not going to interfere in her life."

Energy surged through Falcon, a new fresh energy he hadn't felt in ages. Maybe ever. Was it hope? Acceptance of who he was? "I'm going to go to Boston, then."

Brody smiled and nodded. "I figured as much. I'm not sure she's going to move back here, though. Your dream of a life with Bella on the ranch might not be a possibility. You might have to choose."

Falcon glanced at the horizon again, at the horses, at the land where the only family he had lived.

"Plus, she's not the same person you've been dreaming of for ten years, the sixteen-year-old with a crush on you."

Falcon nodded. "Yeah, I know. I'm not the same either."

"No, you're not." Brody regarded him. "I love you, Falcon, and I love my sister. I want both of you to find happiness, but I'll be honest, I don't know that the two of you fit each other. You've lived in a world of darkness, revenge, and isolation for a long time. Bella isn't in that place. She's not that person. You can't drag her into your darkness. You have to rise up out of it to meet her."

Falcon ground his jaw. "I know who she is."

"She's more than what you've let yourself see. She's light, love, and laughter."

Light. Love. Laughter. God, that sounded good to Falcon. "I have an app on my phone that will fake a laugh for me, so I don't have to."

Brody raised his brows, and then grinned. "Shit. You had me for a second. I actually believed you."

Falcon laughed then, a real laugh that felt good. "I'm ready for all that lightness, Brody. I need it."

Brody inclined his head. "Don't expect Bella to save you.

It's not fair to her. Save yourself and then meet her on equal footing."

Falcon nodded. "Yeah, I know." He hadn't thought about it before Brody had brought it up, but he knew Brody was right. He couldn't ask Bella to save him. She deserved more than that.

"Don't settle for less than what Tatum and I have," Brody said. "You'll have to put the fantasy out of your head and see Bella and yourself for who you are today. And admit it if it's not right."

Falcon laughed softly. "Twenty years later, and you're still preaching."

"Of course I am. I'm a happily married man deliriously in love with his wife. It gives me street cred." But Brody was grinning. "One more word of advice?"

"Sure."

"Take a couple days here before you rush after Bella. Get some food. Get some sleep. Wash your clothes. Take a shower. Ground yourself. You smell like a sewer and look even worse. She'll probably shoot you before she has a chance to recognize you."

Falcon looked down at himself. "I think it shows true love to go like this."

Brody raised his brows. "Bella doesn't want love, remember? The last thing that'll work for you is to show up there desperate, hungry, and dirty with a dozen roses." He put his hand on Falcon's shoulder. "Take a breath, bro. Just take a breath."

Falcon inhaled deeply, but it didn't calm his restlessness. "I need to go. Can I take one of the jets?"

Brody sighed. "You're going to fuck it up before you even get a chance."

Dammit. He'd waited so long. He didn't want to blow it.

"At least take an hour for food, a shower, and some clean clothes. You can't get on my plane smelling like that."

17

"An hour?"

"Yeah."

An hour. He could wait an hour. He'd waited ten years for Bella. What was one more hour?

An eternity, but also, nothing. Not to him. Not anymore. "All right. Feed me, bro. I'm starving."

FOUR

A MEAL, a shower, and a plane ride later, Falcon pulled his rental into the parking lot of the Cape Cod estate where Brody had said Bella would be. It was almost midnight, and the parking lot appeared to be emptying out. The last remaining guests were wandering out to their luxury cars, dressed in high fashion. Women had their hair perfectly done, and they were decorated with jewels. They were laughing, smiling, giggling, chatting.

He parked his truck and leaned back in his seat, watching the exodus of people who definitely showered more than once a week, ate regular meals, and were able to socialize on a normal level. "Hell."

This place was pure class. Upscale. Everything he wasn't, and never wanted to be.

Definitely not the place for a rogue loner who hadn't showered or eaten in days.

Or even one who had.

He wrapped his hands around the steering wheel, flexing his hands.

What the fuck was he doing, walking into a place like this?

Being stupid.

And going after what he wanted. Or at least testing the waters.

He needed to know if he had a chance. If romance was forever impossible with Bella, he'd walk away. She'd never know how he felt, and she'd never have to feel awkward around him when they ran into each other in the future.

But if there was a chance, even a ghostly sliver of a chance, he had to know.

And he had to know *now*, because now was the first time he'd had the chance to start his life.

Without Bella, he had no idea what that life would look like.

And even with her, he still had no idea what life would look like. He knew nothing about who he had to be now, but he did know how he felt about her.

How he'd always felt about her.

Falcon took a deep breath, then forced himself to open the door and step out. He inhaled the night air, which tasted like ocean salt and sea spray. He could hear music drifting around from the back of the estate, so he headed around that way.

The grass was perfectly manicured, and the landscaping was beautiful. He appreciated the flowers. Someone who knew what she was doing, and cared about it, had spent a lot of time and money making the grounds gorgeous.

His mom had liked flowers, and he still thought of her when he saw something like this masterpiece.

The flowers made him feel like she was there with him, and he relaxed slightly and began to whistle an old song from his childhood. The tune made him relax even further, and this time, his deep breath actually sank into his cells, slowing down time.

He slowed his gait, centering himself as he walked along the stone path beside the main building on the estate. Brody was right. Falcon knew that Bella wasn't interested in dating or falling in love. He had to give her that space, not haul ass around the corner and throw himself at her feet.

He grinned at the visual. Who knew? Maybe it would work. Bella had never been predictable.

Falcon rounded the corner, and paused at the sight of the tables and chairs spread across the lawn, looking over the bluff down to the ocean. A few couples were dancing, twinkling white lights sparkled around the edges of a big tent, and there was so much laughter.

Female laugher.

He realized that most of the people still there were women, and they were having a hell of a time.

Falcon scanned the tent, looking for the one face he'd come to see.

Not her.

Not her.

Not her…

Her. His gut seemed to freeze when he saw Bella across the tent from him.

God, she was beautiful.

It had been ten years since he'd met her, and she still took his breath away every time he saw her. It didn't even matter what she was wearing. He usually didn't even notice.

He just fell into her smile, her blue eyes dancing with laughter, the way she always seemed ready to start dancing, no matter what she was doing.

She was looking at Piper, telling a story with such animation that her free hand was moving quickly. He couldn't discern her words, but her voice drifted through the night, wrapping around his heart.

He felt like it was the first time he'd really heard her, really seen her. He'd kept himself on lockdown for so long, and now, suddenly, he was free to notice her, to talk to her, to connect with her.

To admit how much he cared.

FIVE

BELLA FINISHED HER STORY, laughing so hard she could barely tell it. What a night it had been! Chaos had reigned supreme, and her meal hadn't been up to her standards, and no one had cared. The night had been so full of love, and that was all that mattered.

She'd adored the energy flowing through the party, and a little part of her had watched with envy to see all these people caring so much about each other.

She wanted to be a part of it. Of a life like that. A life of possibility. Of futures that were exciting and unpredictable.

This was where she wanted to be. In Boston. Away from the ranch. From horses. From all the stories of her past that she could never seem to escape.

Here, no one knew her. She was just the caterer, a friend of Piper and Kitty. No one had realized she was Bella Hart, because it was her brothers who were always in the spotlight, while she and Meg had stayed on the ranch, living small, playing safe.

No one would have expected Bella Hart to be serving them coffee, so although she'd gotten a few second looks, no one had noticed that it was her in the kitchen.

She hadn't felt like herself tonight. Instead, she'd felt like a woman who had no past, a woman who could have any future she chose, a future that didn't carry a thousand shadows with it. She felt like a blank slate who could run anywhere and do anything, and no one would notice, and no one would care.

It was terrifying and glorious at the same time. Where did she want to run? She didn't even know.

All she knew was how she wanted to *feel*, which was exactly how she was feeling right now. Free. Connected with women. No longer connected to everything that had made her who she was today.

Piper paused, looking past Bella. "That is one good-looking man. He looks like danger, sex, and all sorts of rule breaking. I didn't see him earlier. You think we should call security?"

"Who?" Bella twisted around, scanning the room. "Where?"

"The guy in the black leather jacket and jeans. He's on the stone walkway that circles around to the front of the estate."

Bella followed Piper's instructions, and her gaze landed on the man her friend was talking about.

His face was in shadow, but he was every bit the raw danger vibe that Piper had mentioned. Goosebumps pricked up on her arms, and recognition pulsed at her. Recognition of a kindred soul, someone who had lived in violence their whole life? Someone who was everything she didn't want to be anymore.

But something about him was absolutely riveting. He *was* danger, and a part of her wanted to march over there, throw herself at him, and breathe in every dangerous thing he'd ever done.

"Bella?" Piper said, amusement in her voice. "You want a napkin to wipe the drool off your chin? I'm sure we have one around here somewhere."

Bella cleared her throat and turned away, rolling her eyes. "I'm not drooling."

"You definitely were. Invisible drool, but drool nonetheless." Piper grinned. "You like dangerous men?"

Oh, Lordy. "I definitely don't." She did, though, didn't she? She was going to have to get over that.

"We all do, Bella," Piper said, grinning as Bella turned her back on him. "What woman wants a wuss who can't keep up with her? No one. I bet he can shoot a gun. He has that vibe."

"I can shoot my own gun, so I don't need a man who can shoot. I don't need a man at all. I don't date."

"I didn't either, and then I got a fake fiancé and he messed up all my single-woman vows."

Bella grinned as she shifted the platter of coffee mugs she'd been carrying back to the kitchen. "Your Declan is special."

"He is," Piper agreed. "Question: if that smoking volcano of testosterone and danger was walking over here looking at you, would you want me to tell you?"

Bella felt her cheeks heat up. "Nope. I don't care. I don't notice men."

"Bella." Piper's voice became low, edged with alarm. "I know that you, like all the rest of us, have a past that isn't great. I need to know if the man walking toward you like you're his mission is that kind of problem for you. Declan is around here somewhere, and we will all step in to stop him, but I need to know right now."

Fear shot through Bella. She dropped the tray on the table and spun around. The man was indeed striding right toward her. He was silhouetted by the floodlights, and all she could see were his broad shoulders and narrow waist.

Piper tapped her shoulder. "Bella?"

Sudden relief rushed through her. "I know that walk. I know him. It's Falcon." Falcon. The man of mystery in her life. He was never around, and then he would appear like a ghost, then fade off into the darkness again.

It was just like him to suddenly show up in the middle of a party she was catering at a place she'd never been before in her life. How did he always know where to find her? It was one of his many talents. She waved her arms. "Falcon," she called out. "Over here!"

"Falcon?" Piper peered at him. "Holy shit. It is. I didn't even recognize him. He's lost so much weight."

"He has?" Bella didn't have time to notice, because suddenly Falcon was there. He swept her up in a hug, and she burst out laughing, so happy to see him as he spun her around. Sometimes when he showed up, he had so many shadows in his eyes that she'd wanted to hug him.

Otherwise, he was sassy and fun, and made her laugh so hard her sides would ache.

"I've searched the world for you, my princess," he said as he put her down.

She grinned up at him, then her smile faded. His eyes were hooded and unreadable. Shadows. "You all right?"

"Yeah. I am." He paused, as if he were going to say more, then his gaze went to Piper. "Good to see you, Piper. How's married life treating you?"

"Amazing. How is life hiding in shadows and coming out only to rescue women who need help?"

His gaze flicked to Bella, then back to Piper. "It's all right."

"A man of many words, as always." Piper pointed at the tables. "If you're feeling the need to be useful, we're starting to load up the tables. Feel free to jump in."

"Will do. In a sec." He took Bella's hand, his fingers rough and warm as they wrapped around hers.

Falcon had grabbed her hand hundreds of times over the last ten years, but this time, it felt different. This time, Bella noticed the warmth of his hand, and she thought she felt his thumb linger on her palm.

She had to be imagining it. There was no spark between them. He'd extinguished that spark soundly when she was a sixteen-year-old lost teenager and she asked the gorgeous rebel to take her virginity.

Yes, she'd actually asked him to do that.

Thankfully, he'd politely declined the offer. He'd told her he wasn't interested in her like that, and neither of them had ever mentioned it again. And he'd made sure to never give off anything other than the most non-sexy vibes possible when he was around her.

Until…now?

He pulled her to the side. "I need to talk to you."

Her heart started racing. "What's wrong? Is my family in danger?"

"No. Nothing's wrong. I—" He stopped, searching her face.

"What?"

"I… Fuck."

"*What?* Just say it, Falcon. You're freaking me out."

He paused again, then swore. "I need a place to crash for a few days. You got room?"

She stared at him. "You're a billionaire, like the rest of us. You could buy a mansion in cash. But you need to crash at my place for a few days?"

He met her gaze, and didn't look away. "Yes."

Oh, Lordy. The man was still too handsome for words. He took her breath away, just as he had when she was sixteen. Why was he looking at her so intently? "Why?" She frowned. "Am I in danger?"

"Only from me."

Again, the edge to his words. Was she imagining it? Or was he teasing? Why was this vibe feeling so unsettling right now? "Am I in danger from you?"

"No." He answered immediately. "You're never in danger from me. Ever. I swear."

She frowned at his answer. He sounded so serious. "I was teasing. You'd sacrifice your life for me. I know that." She cocked her head. "Why are you being so weird right now?"

He let out his breath and looked away, staring across the ocean. "I can't say."

"Ah." She knew he carried secrets that he never shared with anyone but Brody. Secrets about his past. It was his past that kept him on the run, in and out of their lives. Maybe he just wanted company. A friend. Connection. A place he could be himself. "Sure," she said quickly. "I'm renting a little one-bedroom cottage just down the beach. You can have the couch if that's okay."

His gaze shot to hers. "The couch would be great."

She realized her hand was still in his, and suddenly her fingers felt hot. "All right." She wiggled her fingers, and he immediately released her hand, leaving her with a surprising sense of loss for a split second.

Geez. What was wrong with her? Why was she reacting to him like this? "You can head there now, and I'll meet you after we finish cleaning up."

He shook his head. "I'll stay and help."

"Great." She wiggled her shoulders, unsettled by his intensity. He brought back so many memories she didn't want, but at the same time, he felt good to be near. He always had. "Grab some tables, strong guy. I'm taking dishes back to the kitchen."

"You got it. And thanks."

She nodded, and touched his cheek. "We're always here for each other, Falcon. You know that."

"I do know that." He paused. "In case I forget to tell you later, you look beautiful tonight, Bella. You always take my breath away, but tonight, you made me feel like I could breathe for the first time in a very long time."

She stared at him, sudden heat prickling over her skin. "Are you making a pass at me, Falcon? Is that why you're here? To take me up on the offer from when I was sixteen?" She blurted out the question, half teasing, and half not.

His eyes narrowed. "I'd never hold you to an offer you made when you were sixteen." He took her hand off his cheek, and kissed her palm. "I'm going to move some tables. See you soon."

He walked away, leaving her staring after him in surprise.

He'd only answered the last question she'd asked.

The first question? About whether he was there to make a pass at her? He'd ignored it.

Why? Because he felt like his answer had encompassed that?

Or because he knew it hadn't.

Holy crap.

SIX

"GIRLFRIEND, he was definitely looking at you like he wanted to have his wild way with you," Piper whispered.

"He's a family friend. There's no way." Bella's elbow bumped the container of hot fudge, and she swore as she caught it. She was so on edge. Falcon had been everywhere she turned tonight, always close, always watching. There was something different about him, and all her joy of the evening had vanished.

She felt like she was back home on the ranch, watched by her brothers, haunted by her past. Falcon knew so much about her, that the past she was trying to walk away from seemed to crawl across her skin again now that he was here.

The door to the walk-in freezer opened, and Keira and Tori squeezed in.

"We can't think of a better place for girl talk?" Tori asked as she pushed a crate of potatoes to the side. "It's freezing in here."

"It's Falcon," Piper said. "He's running around out there like a little mouse, in every corner. He'll definitely find us and hear us if we talk out there."

"Why is that bad?" Keira asked. "We're talking about him?"

"Obviously," Piper said. "We need a vote. Does it seem like he's interested in Bella?"

Bella felt her cheeks heat up as both Keira and Tori stared at her.

Tori cocked her head, then gave a slow nod. "That might explain the weird vibe I'm getting from him."

"Right!" Bella threw her hands up. "I wasn't imagining it, was I?"

"No." Tori paused. "You think he's undressing you with his very hot mind?"

"I think he is," Piper said. "You can feel the heat rolling off him. He can't take his gaze off her."

"I did see him check out your ass," Tori said.

"Oh, God. He did *not*." Bella put her hands on her butt in defense of her curves. "There has never been a romantic spark. Ever."

"I think he's had a change of heart," Piper said. "How do you feel about that?"

Bella leaned back against the cold metal wall, her mind whirling. "No." The response was automatic. "Absolutely not."

"That's an emphatic no." Tori nodded with understanding. "Just Falcon, or any man?"

"Any, but especially him."

"Why especially him?" Keira was leaning against one of the shelves, playing with a carrot.

Bella looked around at the women huddled in the cold freezer with her. She didn't know them that well. They were best friends with Maddie, who had married Bella's brother, so she'd gotten to know them, but they weren't her people, not really, as much as she wanted them to be.

They didn't know her past. All the shadows that Bella could never escape. She knew they wouldn't betray her to the press, leak a story for a few bucks, but the habit of never trusting anyone outside her family was so deep.

She realized then as she stood in that freezer that she couldn't let them in. She didn't know how. Not really. So she shrugged, suddenly wanting to shrink into the cold metal behind her.

Tori's face softened. "It's okay, Bella. We all have secrets. We all have pasts that make us wish we had a magic eraser so we could simply make it vanish."

Piper smiled. "You guys all know mine. It's such a relief not to be hiding anymore."

Bella could imagine it was. And a magic eraser? Damn. She would give up all her billions to be able to use that on her past. Not on her Hart family, though. She'd keep every vivid memory she had before she'd give up her family, which she'd gotten because of her past.

Le sigh.

Keira put her arm around Bella and kissed her cheek, a gesture so sweet that Bella suddenly wanted to cry. "You don't need to tell us anything, Bella. But if you don't want Falcon to stay at your house, tell him."

Tori nodded. "Boundaries, girl. You can make them all pretty and fancy, like red silk rope with pretty tassels and some diamonds sprinkled in there, but they're still bound-aries and you're still in charge of who you let in."

"If he's wanting to stay at your place so you can shoulder his manly issues, then you don't need to do that either," Piper said. "You just don't."

"Right?" Keira rolled her eyes. "He just shows up suddenly in your life and wants a couch? Who does that?"

"I did that," Tori said. "I totally did that to you. And you let me sleep there."

Keira grinned. "Yes, but you didn't bring an overload of testosterone into my house. You brought bestie energy. Totally different."

"Right?" Tori raised her brows at Bella. "Want me to ask for your couch tonight? And then you can just tell him that girls trump boys, and he's not invited."

"Oh! I'll stay too," Keira said.

"I'm not staying at her house," Piper said. "I have a hot ball of testosterone waiting for me tonight. I love you guys, but I can't give up a night of that deliciousness."

"See?" Tori said. "This is why I'll never date again. One whiff of that aftershave and boom, a girl forgets everything that makes her strong, powerful, and badass."

Bella felt her tension ebbing as she listened to the three women banter. They were so funny, so nice, and two of them were as committed to being single as she was. She took a breath. Maybe these were her people. Maybe she could become besties with them. Right? Maybe? She wasn't so broken, was she?

The door suddenly opened, and Meg popped her head in. "Wow. There are a lot of women in here." She grinned. "Bella, I'm hitting the road. I want to get back to the ranch tonight."

Tori raised her brows. "You know Falcon well. What do you think?"

"Oh, no, no." Bella quickly moved past the women and grabbed her sister's arm. "They just want you to score his hotness, which we can't because we know him too well. I'll just walk you out. See you gals!" She pulled Meg out of the fridge and escorted her toward the door. "Thanks for coming out."

Meg stopped. "What's going on?"

"Nothing—"

"Liar. You're a Hart. You can't lie to a Hart. It's against the law."

Bella sighed. "Not here."

"Here. Now. You know how it festers. This is a fester-free zone." Meg leaned in. "You know that it will get better if you put it out into the Hart Universe so I can belittle it until we're both laughing through our tears."

Bella smiled. "We've had a lot of tears."

"And laughter." Meg tucked her arm though Bella's. "Release the fester, sis. Set it free."

Bella started laughing. "All right." She looked around and didn't see Falcon. She lowered her voice. "Falcon asked to crash on my couch."

Meg nodded. "Okay."

"And I don't know if I'm okay with that."

Her sister looked at her with sudden amusement. "Is sixteen-year-old Bella having a fan girl moment?"

"No, but…he's being weird. And the girls said…they said he was checking out my butt. They think he's into me."

Meg's eyes widened, but unfortunately, she didn't laugh it off. "What do you think?"

"Maybe."

"Holy crap." Meg took a step back. "*Holy crap, Bella.* Falcon is…." She didn't need to finish. They both knew who he was.

Dangerous.

A loner.

Uncommunicative.

And loyal. So damned loyal. He'd always shown up when he was needed by the Harts. Every. Single. Time.

Meg leaned in. "If he were into you, would you be interested?"

"No. I'm trying to get away from my past, not lean into it."

Her sister let out a low whistle. "I'll tell you one thing. Don't mess with him. If you're not interested and he is, tell him straight up."

"And if he's not interested, but I give him the speech?"

Humor glinted in Meg's eyes. "He'll probably be afraid to

ever speak to you again, he'll be so scared of giving you the wrong impression again. That won't work."

"No." Bella saw Falcon walk in from the patio. "Here he comes. We're all done here. What do I tell him about crashing on my couch?"

Meg followed her gaze. "What do you want to tell him?"

"I—" Bella paused. She'd been about to say she wanted to tell him no, but just as she was about to say it, he saw them, and flashed them a smile. His trademark devilishly sexy smile that made her belly flip every single time she saw it. "It's complicated."

"It sure is." Meg waved as Falcon neared them. "Hey, Falcon. I'm going to jump on the jet and head back to Oregon. You want a ride?"

His gaze went to Bella. "If you don't want me to stay with you, just tell me."

Dammit. Everyone in her life was much too observant.

She took a breath. "Honestly, I'm feeling conflicted about it. I came out here to forget about my past. To try to find out what it would be like to be someone other than Bella Hart."

His brows shot up. "Bella Hart is pretty fucking awesome."

"I agree," Meg said.

Bella's throat tightened. "Thanks, guys. I just—"

"I don't need to stay. It's fine." Falcon's gaze was shuttered, unreadable. "I'll be in the area for a few days though. Text me if you need anything. Otherwise, I'll see you around." And with that, he gave them the typical Falcon nod and then turned around and strode across the ballroom, heading toward the patio.

"That man is an enigma," Meg said as they watched him leave. "He keeps everything so locked down. I have no idea if he's into you romantically or not, but he was pretty adamant about how awesome you are. As your sister, I appreciate that."

Bella watched him walk out of sight, around toward the front of the estate.

"Question for you, Bella," Meg said.

"What's up?"

"If he were interested in you, is there any chance at all that you might want to follow that path? Because if there is even the tiniest chance, then I think you need to consider that you might never have this opportunity again. Falcon doesn't reach out often, and we both know that."

Bella looked at her sister, her heart starting to race. "If I said he could crash on my couch, it doesn't mean anything, right?"

"It doesn't mean anything unless you both decide it does."

Bella watched Falcon disappear from view. "All I want is to start a different life," she whispered. She felt so desperate for change that she could barely breathe. "He's only my past."

"At the moment, yes, but he could be your future."

"I don't want that future," she whispered.

"Then there's your answer." Meg put her arm around her. "I love you, Bella. Don't question your choice. Believe in yourself, and know that I love the heck out of you, as do all the rest of the Harts. As does Falcon. You'll never lose that, no matter what path you take. You know that, right?"

Bella nodded. "I know." She looked at Meg. "I gotta go."

Then she took off running across the ballroom to go get Falcon before he drove away.

SEVEN

FALCON CHANGED his mind and headed toward the ocean instead of his truck.

He found the stairway down to the water, and decided to be civilized and use them instead of slamming his way down the dune. He jogged down the steps, his boots thudding on the weathered boards.

He reached the sand and strode to the water's edge, letting the low tide hit his boots.

Eyes closed, he raised his arms up, breathing in the salt air, the ocean breeze, the roar of the surf.

Bella was lost to him.

He'd waited too long.

She didn't even want him on her couch as friends. *Fuck.* Did he not even have her as a friend anymore? He was that tainted?

His timing had sucked.

He should have listened to Brody.

He'd spent the last twenty years learning to listen to his instincts, his guides, and he'd thrown himself into this situation without listening to Brody, without getting the green light from his guides.

He'd just run as fast as he could toward Bella in the very moment she would want him the absolute least.

Maybe she was right to cut him off.

If she really wanted nothing to do with the ranch anymore, with her past, what did he have to offer? All he had was their past. He had no idea what his future would be. Could be. Should be.

She wanted fun and laughter. He didn't even know what that was anymore.

He shoved his hands in his pockets and stared across the ocean.

As he stood there, his hands began to burn.

His palms more specifically.

No.

No.

No.

He immediately turned away and began walking down the beach.

His hands kept burning.

Shit.

He hunched his shoulders, bent his head, and walked faster, like he was shoving his way through a thick sludge.

Before he knew it, he was running, sprinting down the beach, racing away from whatever was making his hands burn, from the future he didn't have, from everything he was.

He kept running, harder, faster, an all-out-sprint. His legs burning, the ocean splashing up under his feet, his lungs aching.

He ran until he couldn't breathe, until he finally dropped to his knees and shoved his hands into the wet sand. He knew he hadn't run that far, but he'd run so fast that he'd burned himself out.

Maybe a mile. Or two. Three? He had no idea.

He let the cold, wet sand ease the burning in his hands, hoping it would stop.

Eventually it always did. Then the headache would come, but he could live with the headache.

He bowed his head. Waiting for it to ease.

"Falcon?"

He bolted to his feet, staggering to keep his balance. He spun around and saw Bella standing on the deck of a little house above the beach. She was wearing the same outfit that she'd been wearing at the party. "What are you doing here?" he asked.

"This is the cottage I rented," she said. "What's wrong?"

"Nothing." He almost started laughing to himself. Of course, he had to run toward her house and run out of gas right in front of it.

"Why were you down on your knees looking like you're about to die?"

"I never look like I'm about to die." He stood taller, trying to slow his breathing, but he'd run himself into the ground, so it was a little tricky.

She leaned on the railing. "It's fate, you know."

"What is?"

"That you ran here. I went after you to tell you it was all right for you to crash on my couch, but you'd disappeared." She smiled. "I had no idea you were going to run the beach and meet me here. My bad. Totally missed that."

Stunned relief shot through him. *Hell, yeah.* He shrugged. "Yeah, don't know how we didn't have clear communication on that one."

"Where's your overnight bag?"

"In my truck. I was going to run here, run back there, get my truck, and then drive here. It seemed like the simplest way to do it."

"Absolutely." She waved. "All right. I'm going in. I'll see you when you're back." Then she turned, walked back into the cottage, and shut the door.

Falcon stood there staring after her, then he broke into a

grin. *Hell, yeah.* He sent up a quick thanks to the stars, and then turned and began to jog back down the beach.

Bella snuck back onto the deck, watching as Falcon jogged down the beach again.

She chuckled as she watched him. He was literally going to run back and get his truck. He could have asked for a ride, but he hadn't.

Because the man never asked for help on anything.

She leaned on the railing, watching him go.

He was so athletic. He was leaner, she realized, just like Piper had said. But as he ran, there was something lighter about him. Something…different.

Maybe it wasn't that he was thinking of her naked.

Maybe it was something else.

Did she want him thinking of her naked? No. Yes. No. Yes. Dammit.

She smacked her hands on the railing.

She was definitely going to have to be asleep before he got back. She'd leave the door open, put the sheets out for him, and then be asleep.

But as she headed inside, she couldn't help but smile.

She was glad he was crashing on her couch. Why was she glad?

Because he felt like home. Nothing else.

With Falcon on her couch, she could get a touch of home while still being free to figure out who she was.

That was it.

Nothing else.

He was home in a non-pressure way.

He definitely wasn't six-pack abs, corded thighs, and broad shoulders.

Definitely not.

EIGHT

THE NEXT MORNING, Falcon was halfway through cooking the pancakes when Bella's door opened. His stomach tightened at the sight of her standing there in sweatpants and a tee shirt, bare feet, and tousled hair. God, she was beautiful.

Not that he was going to make the mistake of saying that again.

She rubbed her eyes. "You made breakfast?"

"I did." He gestured to the table he'd set on the deck. "I figured the chef doesn't get people cooking for her very often so I thought I'd offer my culinary services as a thanks for the couch."

Bella smiled and shuffled into the kitchen. "And coffee?"

"Always coffee." He poured her a cup and slid it across the counter. "How'd you sleep?"

She ignored the table outside on the deck and scooched onto a barstool at the kitchen island. "You seem different. What's going on?"

He raised his brows.

"And before you say nothing, remember the Hart rule."

"I'm not a Hart." He had to make that very clear. Even

40

though none of the Harts were biologically related, siblings by heart were still siblings, and he was definitely outside that.

She cocked an eyebrow at him. "You're going to try that? Inner circle rules still apply."

He grinned. "You and I both know that I don't listen to that rule."

"You do with Brody."

"This is true. Brody is like a mama wolverine. I'm scared of him."

She giggled. "He would love being called a mama wolverine. I feel like that fits him."

Ah...her giggle. He'd been searching for that. "I'm not sure which would make him happier. Being called a mama or a wolverine."

"Both, I'm sure. Putting them together is the magic ingredient though. Fierce and protective. It's him."

"It is." Falcon handed her a plate of pancakes. "The pancakes will lose their magic if they get cold. Eat 'em up."

She wrinkled her nose at him. "I haven't forgotten my question, so don't be thinking you're some sly manipulator. But I do like hot pancakes."

"Exactly. Why sacrifice perfect pancakes just to harass me, when you can harass me in ten minutes after eating the amazing pancakes?"

She grinned as she accepted the plate. "I don't know. It can be highly satisfying to harass you. Hot pancakes might be worth the sacrifice, if I weren't so hungry."

He relaxed. Their banter was returning. "You'll be a much better harasser on a full stomach."

"You're right. I need to be at my best." She stood up and grabbed her coffee. "I'm going to the deck to fuel up. I'll let you know when I'm ready to resume my interrogation."

"Can't wait. I'll get your utensils." He whistled under his breath as he followed her outside. All right. He knew his approach now. He just had to be normal, and see where it went. Keeping her as a friend was most important, so he had to start there.

Friends. Laughter. Fun.

Easy.

Except for the fact he couldn't stop thinking about more.

Bella leaned back in her seat, sated and happy. The beach was starting to fill up with people, the sun was bright, and the sky was blue. Falcon had gotten into one of his silly moods, and he'd had her laughing until her sides hurt with his stories about his adventures.

He seemed so normal now. He was Happy Falcon, and she loved that side of him.

Did she really want to make him talk about whatever had been weighing on him earlier?

Not really.

But he leaned forward, and his smile faded. Her heart started to pound. "You've got that serious look, Falcon."

He grinned. "Sorry. I just wanted to ask you a question."

She bit her lower lip. The current in the air had changed suddenly. They were outside, but it felt like the air was vibrating with energy, tension, heat. And to her surprise, she liked it. So she raised her brows. "What's the question?"

"What's next for you? Brody and you both mentioned you wanted to get away from the ranch. He isn't sure you're ever coming back. What's up?"

She let out her breath. "I don't know," she said honestly. "When I came out here and met Maddie and her friends, I felt this...longing? I'm not sure. It just made me realize that I've been living in this little world on the ranch, and I wanted more."

He nodded. "I get that. What do you want?"

She held out her hands, palms up. "Empty."

He studied her hands for a moment, then nodded again. "You have no idea. You just know you've been stuck and it's time to move in a new direction."

Relief rushed through her. "Yes, exactly." She sighed. "I was able to help out with the catering last night, and I loved being a part of all those amazing women, but honestly? I didn't love cooking. I've been doing it on the ranch for so long, it felt like more of the same. Different place, different people, but still me in a kitchen."

He narrowed his eyes. "No cooking then. Lots of women and female bonding."

She rubbed her chin. "I guess, yes. I mean, don't we all want friends?"

"We all want belonging," he agreed. Hence the reason he wanted to move to the Hart ranch and park himself there. The Harts were the only people he had ever fit. Oh, and the Stocktons, the family that the Harts were now also related to by marriage. "You have the Harts and the Stocktons. Lots of women in the Stockton clan these days. Not enough?"

She grimaced. "I'm sure I sound very ungrateful, and I'm not. I do love them. I have this giant family. I guess I just feel like I've fallen into it on autopilot. I never really chose this life. I want something in my life to be something I chose for me, because it lights me up. Like purpose work. Have you heard people talk about that?"

He nodded. "It's your heart purpose. What you came to this life to do."

"Exactly." She sat back. "I don't have a purpose. I just cook for people paying a lot of money for a dude ranch vacation, and then I hang out on a ranch. I mean, I love it. I do. I love my family so much, and I'd do anything for them, but my heart—" She put her hand over it. "It feels like there is more, and I don't know what it is."

He rubbed his jaw. "You're not a bad person for wanting to find what lights you up."

"Sometimes I feel like it." She sat back, gazing across the beach. "I want to wake up in the morning, so excited for my day that I can't even make myself stay in bed. Do you ever feel like that? So excited for life? Feeling like you *matter*?"

"No." He smiled ruefully. "I've been on a journey for twenty years, and it ended yesterday. I have no reason to get up anymore. I don't know what or who I am without it."

For a moment, Bella was too surprised to respond. Falcon never opened up with her. Ever. He always kept a slight distance between them, but the edge to his tone told her exactly how deeply he'd just let her in. "What journey have you been on?"

He glanced at the ocean, breaking eye contact. "I've been hunting a man for twenty years. I finally found him yesterday."

She blinked. *"Hunting?"*

"Yep. A moral justice mission. I couldn't stop until I killed him."

She stared at Falcon, shocked, but also not at all surprised. There had always been an edge to him. "You killed him yesterday?" To the outsider, that would be a shocking question, but she was a Hart. They all had pasts, and Falcon was no exception.

If Falcon had killed a man, there was a reason. But regardless of the reason, killing a man in cold blood would haunt him forever.

He shook his head. "No. He was dead when I got there."

She let out her breath. "Oh, thank God."

"I wanted to kill him."

"And a part of you was also relieved you didn't have to." When Falcon looked over at her, she smiled. "I've known you for a long time, Falcon. You have an amazing, beautiful heart full of love. There is no way you really wanted to kill another person, but you would do what it takes to protect those you love. I'm glad you don't have to live with that."

He bent his head, looking down at his hands. He didn't speak for a long time.

As they sat there, she finally understood why he seemed so different. He *was* different. Whatever had happened with that man had ended, and that left him…lost. Like her. "Is that all you've done for twenty years? Hunt for him? Is that why you always disappeared for extended periods of time?"

"Yeah." He was still staring at his hands. He turned them so his palms were up, and he flexed his fingers. "He knew I was hunting him. It was a game to him. He mocked me. And I kept going. I made a promise. I had to finish."

Bella slid her chair around, then leaned toward him and put her hands over his.

He shifted slightly so his head was resting against hers, creating an intimacy that made her heart skip. This man had been her dream for so long. Moments like this were what she'd always longed for. A connection that was deep. Intimate. Powerful.

Why was it happening now? Why *now*, when all she wanted to do was walk away from her history and her stories, with which he was inextricably intertwined?

"Do my palms feel hot to you?" Falcon asked.

She was surprised by the question, but took a moment to experience the feel of his hands against hers. His skin was rough, and her heart seemed to skip a beat as she focused on the sensation of their hands touching. "They feel normal warm. Like you're alive, but not noticeably hot. Why?"

He swore under his breath. "I've seen some weird shit on my trips, Bella."

"Like what?"

He didn't answer, but he closed his fingers around her hands, holding them tightly.

"Falcon," she whispered.

"What?"

"Why did you need to kill that man?"

Again, he didn't answer.

He'd said twenty years. He was thirty years old now. "What happened when you were ten?" Always their childhood. So much trauma that all of them still carried with them.

"You know what, Bella?"

"Tell me." Their cheeks were now resting against each other. If they both turned their heads toward each other, a kiss would be inevitable. But it would take both of them.

"I don't want to live in that world anymore. It's over. I don't want to talk about it or think about it. It's time for me to start living."

She let out her breath. Was it that easy to leave behind a past you didn't want? Was it that easy to step off the road you didn't want to be on, even if you'd been on it for twenty years? "What do you want to do?"

For the third time, he didn't answer.

"Do you know?" she asked.

He squeezed her hands and sat up, pulling away. His absence left a gaping hole for a split second before she pulled herself together.

She sat up and reclaimed her hands. "Too many questions," she said. "Back to being an island, eh?"

He leaned on the railing. "You ever think about getting married, Bella? Having a family? Doing that whole thing?"

"Married? No way."

He raised his brows. "That was emphatic."

"Absolutely." She leaned back in her chair and put her bare feet up on the railing. "I wouldn't know how to be a good mom. So, I don't want any kids to mess up. And as for getting married?" She shook her head. "I don't even want a boyfriend, let alone a husband."

He was watching her closely. "What if he was a really good guy? There are some good ones out there."

"I know there are. Piper and Maddie are married to good

ones, and all the Stocktons. Plus my brothers are all amazing people. It's just not for me."

"Why not?"

She paused, trying to think about how to articulate it. "If you fall in love, then the person you love will want you to be a certain way. And if you love them back, you'll try to fit that mold. And then you lose the chance to find your own way."

He frowned. "How many relationships have you been in?"

"Enough." She shrugged, suddenly restless. "There's so much pressure on women to get married and couple up. Why? Men don't have that pressure. You've been free for twenty years. You probably don't even know what I'm talking about, the need to be free."

"I wasn't free. I was trapped by the promise I'd made. Now, I'm free."

Her heart tightened. Whatever he'd been trying to fix, it had hurt him. She could see it. "I'm glad you're free, Falcon. What are you going to do with it?"

"I want to move to the Hart Ranch," he said quietly. "I want to put down roots. I want to grow a garden. I want to find out what life is like when I'm not running all the damned time." He paused. "I want to get married. Adopt some foster kids who need homes. Create a life I've never had, not even as a kid. Create a family, and make one for others who never had it either."

Her heart seemed to stutter to a full stop for a moment. "You do?" Never in all her life would she have guessed that was Falcon's dream. He'd always been a vagabond. A loner. When she was younger, all she'd wanted was a knight in shining armor to swoop in and take care of her. That need had made her chase a lot of jerks who had shown her that she was better off counting on herself.

"Yeah." He turned to face her. "The opposite of you, I guess. We'd never work."

"Us?" She blinked. "*Us?*"

"Yeah." His fingers tapped the railing restlessly. "Here's the deal, Bella. I came back for you. I want that house on the ranch, but I want it with *you*. I wasn't going to tell you. I was just going to sweep you off your feet. But if you would really never get serious or settle down, if the future I want isn't ever a possibility with you, then I want to know."

She felt like she couldn't breathe. "You want...me?"

"Yeah. Always have. But my life was too dangerous. I don't care if I need to wait another ten years, if there is a chance. But if there will never be a chance, I need to know."

She stared at him, too stunned to speak. "It's... you've...never..."

"I had to keep you safe." He shifted. "What do you say, Bella? Is there a chance you would want to get married some-day? Move to the ranch? Have a family? With me?"

She couldn't believe she was having this conversation. "For *years*, I dreamed of you," she said. "I dreamed you'd come back from one of your trips and take me away from my life. We'd run to New York City. I'd become a fashion designer. We'd go to fancy dinners, and Broadway, and the opera. We'd never set foot on a ranch ever. Never pat a horse. I'd wear a long dress all the time, and you'd wear a tuxedo every day. We'd be so far away from our pasts that they would vanish forever."

His eyes flickered with an emotion she couldn't read. "You wanted me."

"I wanted you to save me with your rippled muscles and moody silence."

He grinned. "I'm not moody. I was silent because if I spoke, I'd do something like ask this sweet young thing to wait for me, even though I might never come back for her."

She sat back and flung her hands in the air. "If you had said that, I would have sat on my front step every single minute for the rest of my life, waiting for you."

He grinned. "I'm not worth that, but that image is great for my male ego."

She rolled her eyes. "You were my imaginary knight in shining armor. I kept thinking you would save me, and when you didn't, I went in search of other men who would."

His smile faded.

She leaned forward. "I would have given anything for a chance with you back then, Falcon, but it would have been a terrible mistake. I needed to find myself and realize how to rescue myself first."

"And now?"

"I've spent my whole life doing the exact opposite, until I got on that plane and flew out here to do the wedding I did last night." She took a breath. "I think that crush on you is still there. I think I would be willing to give up on myself to move back to the ranch to be with you, and that would break me. I can't do that, Falcon."

He nodded slowly. "I couldn't do that to you."

Her heart was pounding. "I can't believe the man I've had a crush on my whole life wants me."

"I can't believe the woman I've dreamed of for years thinks I have rippled abs and a coat of armor."

The air was strung so tightly between them, she felt like she was going to snap. "What now, then?"

He let out his breath. "I'll leave."

Oh, God. She didn't want him to leave. "If you stay, I'll lose myself in you," she whispered.

"I know." He stood up. "I spent twenty years chasing a monster, and I've wondered many times if that quest was turning me into one myself. If I take you away from who you need to be, then I'd know that I'd become exactly what I didn't want to be." He walked over to her, slid his hand under her jaw, and leaned down. "Bella Hart, I have loved you since you were sixteen, and I'll love you 'til I'm gone. For that reason, I'm getting the hell out of here before I become less than the man you deserve."

Then he bent his head and brushed his mouth over hers.

It was a quick kiss, velvet-soft, and she felt like she was plummeting right into his arms.

Then he stepped back, gave her a nod, and walked back into the house.

She didn't move, and it was only a couple minutes before she heard his truck start.

She closed her eyes as she listened to him drive away.

What had she just done? What choice had she just made?

The only one she could have.

NINE

BEFORE BELLA HAD a chance to congratulate herself on her immense discipline and self-love mastery by letting Falcon leave, her phone rang, startling her. Falcon? She pulled it out of her back pocket, then sighed when she saw it was Brody. "Hey," she said, trying to sound cheerful.

"You okay?"

She frowned. "Yes. Why?"

"Where are you?"

She sat up, her heart starting to race at the urgency in his voice. "On the deck of the cottage I rented."

"Do you have your gun on you?"

Bella tightened her grip on the phone. "It's inside. Why? What's going on?"

"Go get it while I talk to you."

Crap. This was why she wanted to get off the Hart Ranch. Because drama followed the Harts everywhere. She just wanted to be normal, or feel normal, for once in her life.

But today wasn't that day, apparently. She instinctively checked the beach as she stood up, carefully assessing everyone in sight. No one felt suspicious, so she turned and headed inside. "Okay. Going to get it. What's up?"

51

"Your house was broken into last night."

Her belly did a little flip. "Was anything stolen?"

"No, but they got in and out without triggering the alarm. Dylan is working on it to figure out how they did that, but it means they knew what they were doing."

She pressed her lips together. "If they didn't take anything, why did they break in?"

"We watched the video. They looked like they were looking for you, and they took their time doing it, like they wanted us to know that they knew they hadn't triggered the alarm, and they had all the time they wanted. When you weren't there, they left. Walked right out the front door and left it open."

Bella's heart started racing, and she hurried into her bedroom and grabbed her gun from her nightstand. She put on her harness and then put the gun on. Then she stood and looked at herself in the mirror.

This was her life. Walking around with a gun.

Sudden tears filled her eyes. *I don't want this life anymore.* "Who was it?"

"We haven't been able to get an ID on them. We can't see their faces. But we're working on it."

"Okay." There were so many possibilities.

"Have you seen Falcon yet?"

Oh. Falcon. "Yes."

"Is he there?"

"Not anymore."

There was a pause that told her that Brody knew why Falcon had come, and therefore knew why he wasn't there anymore. "You all right with him?"

"Of course." She didn't want to get into *that* with Brody.

Brody, fortunately, was too focused on the break-in to press her for details. "Did he tell you anything about what he's been doing for the last twenty years?"

She sat down on the bed, continuing to stare at herself in

the mirror. She looked like a normal woman, except for that freaking gun. And the sadness in her eyes. And those weights on her shoulders.

She had felt basically content on the ranch before meeting Maddie and Piper. Now? She didn't belong anywhere anymore. Meeting them had ripped the veil off her eyes. A part of her wanted to go back to being the Bella who had found peace in her little life on the ranch. Maybe she would have been so happy to dive into Falcon's arms and not think twice about committing to forever on the ranch.

But she couldn't go back, because these women had changed her, and left her with…nothing. Nothing but possibility, right? Just because she didn't know where she was going didn't mean it wasn't going to be wonderful, right? "Falcon said he'd been hunting a man, and he found him dead, so his quest was over."

She almost felt Brody's nod. "Did he tell you what he found in the cabin?"

Oh, God. "No." Did she want to know? No. Yes. No. Yes. "What was it?"

"The dead man had a picture in his hand of you and Falcon. In the cabin were pictures of the rest of the Harts, and the ranch, and plenty of you."

She ground her jaw. "So? He's dead."

"Right, but someone killed him. Who killed him? And do they have any reason to target the Harts and Falcon?"

Of course the journey never ends. "Well, I always carry my gun, so I'm good."

"Bella, these guys were pros. They could take you down easily if you're alone. I know you want to start a life out there, but I'd like to request that you return to the ranch until we get this sorted."

Her heart sank. "Go back home?"

"Just for a little bit. Might be only a few days. Dylan has his team on it. He'll figure it out."

Her brother Dylan was a great investigator with a dangerous team, but she knew that if these guys were good, Dylan would have a challenge. It could take longer than a few days. "If I go back home, I might never leave again."

It had been harder than she'd thought in Boston. She'd thought she'd jump right in, have clarity and purpose, and feel like an empowered, independent free woman. The temptation of the ranch and Falcon's offer was significant.

"When it's over, I'll put you on a plane myself, I promise. I won't let you give up on your dreams."

But what if she forgot her dream? What if being comfortable felt so much better than feeling uncomfortable that she dove right back in, buried her head, and found a way to be content again? "I can't, Brody. I feel like my soul will die if I don't listen to it right now."

He swore under his breath. "Bella, I'm not willing to risk your life. These guys were pros, and I don't know why they were in your house. You can't stay out there alone."

She jutted her jaw out. "You don't control me, Brody."

"I know, but I would never be able to live with myself if I gave you freedom and it got you killed. If I have to be a controlling bastard to keep you alive, I'll do it. You can hate me for life, but at least you'll be hating me from this side of the grave. My job isn't to be your best friend. It's to be your big brother, and the parents you never had."

Hello, Mama Wolverine. "I'm staying in Boston."

Brody swore. "When you're sitting there staring into a gun that's pressed against your forehead, are you going to feel great about that choice, Bella? Are you going to feel like yeah, that was worth the risk?"

Bella pulled out her gun and pointed it at herself in the mirror. She imagined it being a stranger holding that gun, or one of the men from her own past. Chills ran down her spine. She wasn't ready to die. But if she went home, she'd die in a different way. "Can you send a team?"

Even as she said it, her stomach churned. Walking around with a team of armed bodyguards was not the path to feeling normal and free.

"Dylan's team is here, protecting the ranch. We don't know if they'll target one of us. I'm bringing everyone in. Come back."

She lowered her gun. "Brody—"

"I'm sending one of the planes. I'll text you when I know the timing. Be on the plane, Bella. We love you." Then he hung up, pulling rank as the big brother.

She wanted to be mad at him, but she wasn't. He'd kept them all alive as kids. It was what he did, and she appreciated it. They all did. Family was forever, even if they pissed each other off.

Bella dropped the phone onto the bed and stared at herself in the mirror. Her little personal quest for freedom was over already? Trapped as always by the violent pasts that held all the Harts in their shadows. Maybe this was her shadow. Maybe one of her brother's. Maybe Falcon's—

Falcon.

He couldn't be more than a few minutes away.

What if he played bodyguard? Then she could stay, right? He was a complete badass.

Could she handle the temptation of him being around her all the time?

Maybe. Maybe not.

But if she succumbed to him out here in Boston, it was less dangerous than succumbing to him on the ranch.

Besides, she knew he wouldn't let her soul die.

He simply wouldn't.

And neither would she.

TEN

FALCON HIT the gas as he drove away from the beach, flexing his hands on the steering wheel.

He felt weird. Good, weird. Bad, weird.

Good because he'd been able to do something heroic by walking away from Bella. He was impressed as hell with himself.

And shitty as hell because he'd walked away from Bella.

He could have pressed her. When she'd told him how she used to fantasize about him, he'd seen in her eyes that the attraction was still there. He was a temptation for her, and it wouldn't have been that difficult to work his way around her defenses. He could have fought for her.

But when he'd stared into those eyes he'd dreamed of, he'd known he had to be the hero she needed, which meant letting Bella be her own hero.

He let out his breath as he drove.

What the fuck was he going to do now?

The ranch no longer held such an appeal for him, because the ranch had been intertwined with Bella.

So, what now? He had no fucking idea.

The man he'd hunted was dead.

The woman he loved was no longer his to dream of.

The home he'd planned to build was no longer something he wanted in the same way. Live in that house without her? Live in that house alone?

He got to a stoplight and paused. Where was he driving?

No idea.

Literally none.

For the first time in twenty years, he had zero idea of what was next. He didn't even know which way to turn at the stoplight. He didn't even know the next step to take.

He could get gas. Fill up the tank to drive wherever.

That was a step.

He put on his blinker, took the corner, and pulled into a no-name brand gas station that was cash only. Not many of those left on the Cape, he would bet.

He pulled the truck in, started the pump, then leaned back against the side of the truck and clasped his hands on his head, watching the cars go by.

Lots of cars filled with families headed to the beach. Pink inflatables crushed up against the rear window. Screaming kids. Laughter.

He'd had dreams of that. Of crafting that life for kids who thought they'd never have it. Of him and Bella finally learning what it would be like to have a family, learning how to be the parents they'd never had.

He still wanted it.

He absolutely wanted it.

With another woman?

No. He couldn't imagine that.

Without a woman? What if he just fostered some kids and figured it out on his own as a single dad?

Maybe.

Then at least he'd have a purpose. He'd be able to change the trajectory of someone else's life.

The Stocktons had a bunch of foster and adopted kids.

Maybe he'd talk to them. Get some advice. Yeah. He nodded. Yeah, he could do that. He could—

His phone rang, and he contemplated ignoring it.

But he wasn't a man on a quest anymore. He was a man trying to figure out how to become a dad, and dads answered the phone.

It was good practice.

His phone rang again, and he pulled it out of his pocket. His gut dropped when he saw Bella's name on his screen. *What the fuck?* He answered immediately. "Hi."

"I want to hire you."

Hire him? "I'm pretty sure my answer is going to be no." He kept his voice gentle, but he knew collecting a paycheck from her to cart tables around at events wasn't the path he needed.

"Brody said my house got broken into last night by professionals. They were clearly looking for me, and when they didn't find me, they left."

Falcon swore and stood up straight. "Who was it?"

"They don't know. He told me I have to go home until they solve it. He's sending the plane for me. He doesn't think I'm safe enough with my gun and my attitude."

Fuck. Had he brought this on her? "I think he's right." Hell. He was going to have to find out if this was connected with the man who'd ended his quest for him, wasn't he? Back on the road again?

The thought was numbing. He didn't want to go back to that life. He fucking *didn't*.

"If I go back to the ranch, I'll never leave," Bella said. "It's too safe. It's too comfortable. And then my soul will die."

He finished filling his truck, already thinking about what he was going to do first. He'd have to go back to the cabin and look around for—

"Falcon. I want to hire you to be my bodyguard. Brody

58

will trust your ability to keep me safe, and then I can stay out here."

He froze, his hand on the door handle. "Bodyguard?"

"Yes. You're the only one I trust to keep me alive but also not let me betray myself by running home to hide."

He swore again and got in the truck. "I need to find out who's after you."

"Dylan's on it. He's got his whole team. It's what he does. You won't know more than he does."

Falcon hit his fist on the steering wheel. "I'm the one who has to do it. It's my fault—"

"Your fault? You don't even know if it has anything to do with you. You're just making stuff up because you have a hero complex."

He blinked. "A hero complex?"

"Yes. You spent twenty years hunting down one man. Was it worth it? To give up your life? And now you want to do it again, when you don't even know if it has anything to do with you, and Dylan is working on it?"

He gripped the steering wheel. "I don't want to go hunting again—"

"Then don't. Start living, Falcon. That's what I'm trying to do."

"If something happened to you—"

"Because you didn't run off to the mountains and look for some shadow? How about if something happens to me because you did run off, and I refused to go home and I got chopped up by Freddie or Jason or a vampire?"

He started laughing. He couldn't help it. "Freddie?"

"You think I can fend off Freddie myself? He's literally been in a thousand horror movies. He never dies."

"I do think you could handle Freddie, actually. You're a badass."

She paused. "All right, I do, too, but Brody doesn't. I honestly think he'll kidnap me. Will you help me?"

He sighed. Who was he trying to lie to? The thought of being invited to be by Bella's side 24/7 was... *hell, yeah.* But it was a loaded situation. He stared at the cars of families headed to the beach. "I have to be honest, Bella, first."

She paused. "What?"

"I haven't fallen out of my ten-year obsession with you in the last five minutes. If I'm your bodyguard, I need to be within protector reach of you 24/7. And that's going to be tempting as hell."

She was quiet for a moment. "Yeah, for me, too. Now that it's out on the table, it's harder to ignore."

He let out his breath. "Hell, Bella."

He heard her take a deep breath. "It's fine. We can do it. Neither of us want to be broken for the rest of our lives. I'll pay you, and we'll keep it professional. What do you say?"

Bella believed that if they got together, it would leave them both broken for life? *Wow.* That was a statement. Was she right?

"Falcon? Can I call Brody back and tell him you'll be my bodyguard? Please?"

He heard the desperation in her voice, and something inside him softened. She couldn't go back to the ranch right now, and she knew it. Maybe, just maybe, if she took her space now, if she found her identity now, there could be a ranch in her future. Kids.

If Falcon walked away now, there would never be a future for them, because this was their window. He knew it.

If he stayed...maybe there was a chance.

He'd give anything for a chance. Not to leave her broken for life, but for the happiness neither of them had ever found, and they both deserved.

Being by her side would be tempting as hell, for both of them. He wouldn't break her trust...but what if trust could be healed? It was worth everything to take this chance that he'd been given. He had to know what could have been, and if there was anything to fight for now.

"Falcon?"

"Call Brody and tell him I'll do it."

ELEVEN

AS BELLA HUNG up with Brody, barely securing his promise not to land the plane on the beach in front of her cottage and kidnap her, she knew she had to be out of the house today.

She felt too emotional right now with Falcon.

Too emotional being away from home.

Too...everything, and she had no business being behind closed doors with Falcon after he'd told her that he loved her.

Loved her.

Loved her.

So, she called Piper. "Hey, what are you guys up to today?"

"Hey, girl! I was just going to call you. One of our caterers told us she's selling her business, ironically. You want to buy it? You can buy all her contracts and work for us. What do you say?"

What? Bella's hand tightened on the phone. "Are you serious?"

"Yep. I know you were thinking about moving here, and this will give you your foothold. She has a great reputation, and you're a great chef, so it would be an easy transition. I spoke to Kitty about it, and she agreed. We both liked working with you last night, and we'd love to keep going."

Bella sat down at the kitchen table, stunned by the sudden opportunity. "I don't know, I mean, I wasn't sure if—"

"She already has a purchase offer that she is supposed to sign in the morning, but she's holding off for you because I told her you could beat the price, which of course you can. She's catering an event on the Cape tonight, and she said you could stop by. I'll text you the address. Go check it out! This would be such an easy transition for you!"

"Yes!" Kitty took over the conversation. "It's the perfect opportunity. We all love you, and it would be a fantastic way to add to our girl gang. Go meet Diana, fall in love with her business, give her the retirement of her dreams, and start your life. I'll go in on the purchase with you if you want a partner. I love to invest in women, and you are fantastic. Call after you meet with her, and we can discuss. Good? Good. Smooches."

Kitty then hung up, leaving Bella staring at her phone.

What. Just. Happened.

At that moment, she heard footsteps on the back steps, and she looked up as Falcon walked in. His shoulders were wide, and he suddenly seemed too big for the space. He was wearing his cowboy hat, which he hadn't been wearing before, making him look rough, rugged, and delicious.

"You can't leave the door unlocked, Bella," he said as he shut it behind him.

"If someone wants to kill me, a locked door isn't going to stop them."

"No, but if you hear them breaking in, it gives you time to grab your gun and shoot them all first."

Valid point. She held up her phone. "Piper just called. One of their caterers is retiring and they all want me to buy the business, take over all their contracts, and become a part of their girl gang."

His brows went up, but he hid his emotions. "Great for you."

"I don't know if I want that. I literally just got here. Is it trading one safety net for another?"

He pulled out a chair and sat down in front of her, straddling the chair so he could lean on the back of it. "There will be other opportunities."

"Not with contracts already set with Piper and Kitty. I love these women. They're the ones who are inspiring me."

"You don't need to buy their friendship. They will love you just for being you."

Oh, boy. He looked so freaking intense and adorable and interested. And delicious. What would it be like to kiss him? To kiss this man she'd dreamed of for so long? "I forgot how strong my crush on you was, until you told me that you loved me. Now I can't get it out of my head."

His eyes darkened, and he said nothing.

Her words just sat in the air between them, getting heavier and heavier.

Crap. She sat up. "Sorry. I didn't mean to say that. I'm just rattled having you here, rattled by the fact someone broke into my house, and rattled by this offer. A part of me wants to take it, and a part of me is freaking out. I feel like finding your identity should take more than a day, right?"

He let out his breath, a long, slow exhale that she could feel in her soul. He reached over and put his hand on her arm. This time, his palm felt hot, burning her skin. But at the same time, she felt some of her panic ease.

"Better?"

She nodded, surprised to feel her mind settle and her heartrate slow. "Your touch is magical."

He looked down at his hand on her arm, as if he were surprised to see it there. "So I've been told."

What? By whom? Women? Who told him his touch was magical? Did she feel jealous? He was a thirty-year-old attractive man. Of course he had a romantic past. It was none of her business.

But her heart disagreed.

He removed his hand and folded his arms over the back of the chair. "Meet with this woman. Can't hurt. Maybe you'll get some clarity."

"Or maybe I'll be tempted to make a desperate choice."

He regarded her. "I have far more faith in you than that. And you do, too. Just because you're lost doesn't mean you're weak."

She stared at him, and suddenly the fear dissolved. She lifted her chin. This was why she'd needed to step away from the ranch: because she was so used to relying on her brothers to create her world. She wanted to create her own life now, which meant Falcon was right. She needed to trust herself. "All right. I'll meet her."

"When?"

"Tonight. At an event she's catering."

Falcon ground his jaw. "Can you meet with her before? I don't love the idea of trying to keep you safe at a venue where there are dozens of people, and I don't know who to look for."

"I'm not going to hide, Falcon. I've been hiding for so long. I need to be seen in this world. If you don't want to deal with that, you don't have to—"

"No." He interrupted her. "I'm staying. We'll make it happen."

"Okay, great." Conversation faded into silence.

She'd never had trouble talking to him before. Ever.

And now... All she wanted to do was kiss him.

He met her gaze, then suddenly grinned. "You're dying to kiss me, aren't you?"

"I am," she admitted, with a soft laugh. "I literally can't stop thinking about it. I'm in the middle of an identity crisis, a possible assassin situation, and a life-changing business opportunity, and all I can think about is kissing you."

He tipped the chair forward, toward her. "When you called, I'd decided I was going to talk to the Stocktons about fostering some kids. I'd decided to go the single dad route, because you and I were no longer a possibility."

"A dad? You want to be a single dad?" Her heart ached. She didn't want kids. The idea terrified her. His words were such a reminder that the two of them had no path forward together.

"Yeah. I do. I wanted kids with you, but since I can't, I'm doing it alone. I don't want anyone besides you to do it with me."

Her heart turned over. "Falcon—"

He shrugged. "I know we're not compatible with our dreams, but I can't stop thinking about dragging you off that chair, into my lap, and kissing you like you've never been kissed before."

Heat seemed to ignite down her spine. "How are you so freaking hot when you say that?"

"Because I'm a male specimen, of course." He paused. "I won't make a move on you, Bella. Not ever. But if you ever initiate, I won't stop you."

Her mouth suddenly felt dry. "It's more romantic if you sweep me off my feet. Aren't you my knight in shining armor?"

"No, Bella. You're your own knight in shining armor, remember?"

She closed her eyes. "Yes. I know. Yes." It was such a habit to turn her power over to someone else. So much easier. "I'm so used to letting the world spin around me, instead of trying to spin it myself." She opened her eyes. "Even though I'm rich, trained in hand-to-hand combat, and smart, some-times I still feel completely lost and stuck. I could go anywhere, pay anyone to teach me anything, and I keep getting up every day and reliving the same life day after day."

God. When she explained it that way, she felt like such a loser. Not *loser*, but yeah, kind of a loser. An excuse-maker, at least.

"Time to break that rut, eh?"

She nodded. "By buying a catering business and continuing to cook?"

"Only you can answer that."

"I don't know. I'm just…I feel like I'm standing in front of a huge, cement wall, and I can't see what's on the other side, or how to get around it, or even whether I want to."

He studied her. "What's one thing you've always wanted to do, but have never done?"

She rolled her eyes. "A lot of things."

"Name five—No!" He held up his hand. "Name something that you'd be too scared to ever do."

She didn't hesitate. "Sky diving. Parachuting. I don't know why people think that's fun to do?"

He grinned. 'Let's go skydiving today."

"What? No." She sat back. "Absolutely not. No chance."

He raised his brows. "I'm certified. You can tandem jump with me."

"I don't want to. And aren't you supposed to be keeping me alive, not risking my life?"

"What I'm trying to do is help you find your path, so that maybe eventually, you'll be ready to move back home, marry me, and have a family."

She stared at him. "Really?"

"Just kidding. I'd never be that underhanded." His face was deadpan, and she didn't know if he was serious or not. "If you're scared, the best way to break it is to walk right into the fear and out the other side. So do the scariest thing you can think of, and nothing else will feel so scary ever again." Falcon held out his hand. "Come with me. Trust me."

She looked at his outstretched hand. This man had been through hell for twenty years. He knew about fear. He knew about loss. He knew about all the things that haunted her. "Is that what you did? Walked into your fear?"

"Again and again and again." He paused. "Including a few minutes ago when I agreed to be your bodyguard."

She looked at him, and saw the truth in his eyes.

"You're not a wimp, Bella. You've just forgotten your strength for too long." He wiggled his fingers at her. "Come fly with me, Bella."

She didn't want to. At all.

But she also didn't want to keep living the way she was living. She didn't want to walk into that event tonight and buy a catering business because she was too scared to try something else, something new, something that she hadn't even thought of yet.

Maybe Falcon still was her knight in shining armor.

Not because he was going to rescue her.

But because he was going to make her rescue herself. "Fine," she said. "But I reserve the right to back out at any time."

He flashed her a grin. "I saw the perfect place yesterday. It's pretty close."

Of course it was nearby. Less time for her to talk herself out of it.

Falcon caught her chin and lifted her face to his. "Don't look so scared, Bella. The one person I'd give my life for is you, so you can trust that I'll keep you safe. I swear it."

She felt the truth of his words, and she believed him.

On a whim, she leaned in and kissed his cheek. "Thank you. I'll be ready in five minutes."

She turned and bolted for her room before she could be tempted to kiss him again.

And again.

And never stop.

TWELVE

FALCON STOOD in the doorway of the flight shack building, grimly watching Bella as she stood beside the red Cessna, her hands on her hips as she studied it.

She looked like a woman about to give in to her fear, and he wanted to be the guy to tell her not to back down.

And he was going to do the opposite.

Swearing under his breath, he strode across the grassy airstrip. "What do you think?"

"I'm not going up in that plane. It's the size of my tooth-brush. I don't fly my toothbrush up to ten thousand feet, and I definitely don't jump off it strapped to someone else, putting my faith in a parachute packed by some person I've never met."

He ground his jaw. Fear was so debilitating. He wanted to get her out of it. But he couldn't. "Well, then, today's your lucky day."

She looked over at him, hope on her face. "Bad weather? No fuel?"

"No. They won't let me tandem with you. You'd have to jump with one of their instructors."

She raised her brows, studying his face. "You don't like that."

"Nope."

She turned to fully face him. "You're serious."

"Yep."

"Isn't their instructor certified? How difficult is it to jump out of a plane?"

He frowned at her. "You want to go up with a stranger?"

"I don't want to go up at all." She put her hands on her hips. "But I feel like you're being an overprotective zealot not wanting me to jump with someone who is trained."

"I'm your bodyguard. I can't protect you if you jump out of a plane with someone else."

She cocked her head, the corners of her mouth started to curve in a smile. "You think someone is going to shoot me out of the sky?"

"No."

"You think my instructor would sacrifice himself to make me plummet into the ground and become a Bella pancake?" Amusement flickered in her eyes.

He narrowed his eyes. "You're mocking me?"

Her smile blossomed into full bloom. "I am. Yes. A little bit. You gave me this great speech about fear, and now you're telling me I can't jump because I'll be strapped to someone else, and you'll be like twenty feet away from me, in a separate parachute." She leaned into him. "Are you afraid, Falcon? Scared that little Bella can't jump without you?"

He nodded. "Yeah," he said honestly. "I've spent a lot of time in some grisly places in this world, and I know how shit can go south fast. I trust only myself when it comes to my well-being, so that goes double for you."

She stared at him, then sighed. "Damn you, Falcon. Honestly."

"Damn me? Why?"

"Because now I have to jump." She poked him in the

chest. "I'm super pissed at you, because I was going to exercise my right to keep my feet on the ground, but now that you're trying to keep me small and I want to let you, I have to make the opposite choice. I'm not happy about it. At all." Then she shoved past him and marched toward the little cabin where her instructor Ralph was waiting.

"What?" Falcon turned and strode after her. "I'm not going to let you jump, Bella."

She fluttered her hand at him, and he was pretty sure she flipped him the bird. "Now I absolutely *have* to jump. You're banning me? Honest to God, Falcon, you are the worst bodyguard ever. Don't you know by now that if you ban me from doing something, I literally have to do it? That's the life phase I'm in right now. No playing small for Bella."

He caught up to her as she reached the doorway. He caught her arm and turned her toward him. "You don't get to jump with someone else, Bella."

She narrowed her eyes at him, amusement gone from her face. "You don't own me, Falcon. No one does. And I guess this stupid skydiving thing isn't actually about facing my fears. It's about me refusing to let anyone make me play small." She glared at him. "Again, to reiterate, I don't appreciate you being so autocratic that I have to jump. If I die on this jump, I will take my irritation with you to the grave."

Falcon wanted to grin at the same time he wanted to toss her over his shoulder and drag her back to his truck. "Bella," he said quietly. "I'll admit I'm a little bit of a control freak, but it's literally my job to keep you safe. If I'm not strapped to you, I can't control your flight, and I can't keep you safe. We'll find another place."

She raised her chin and looked him in the eye. Then she turned away and spoke to Ralph, a thirty-something man who looked annoyingly capable. "How many times have you jumped in tandem?" she asked him.

His gaze flicked to Falcon, and then he grinned with just a

71

little bit of flippancy. "Over a thousand. I've been jumping for more than ten years."

"Great." She nodded. "And how many times have you crashed?"

His smile widened. "Never."

"How many times have you come close?"

"Zero."

"All right. Let's do it then."

Ralph shot Falcon a look of full-blown amusement before turning his full attention to Bella. "Great, let's get started—"

"Bella." Falcon touched her arm. "No—"

She spun to face him. "I appreciate you want to protect me, Falcon. I do. But I need to be unprotected. You can jump with us, or you can wait on the ground. What do you want to do?"

He swore under his breath, but he saw the determination in her eyes. It was the fire he'd seen in her face when she was a gritty teenager refusing to die in the streets. It had been a long time since he'd seen that fire. He'd be a total ass to try to crush it.

She nodded, clearly sensing his capitulation. "You're jumping with us, then?"

"Yeah."

"Great. Let's do this. Can't wait to find my power."

THIRTEEN

THIS WAS why Bella needed a life without men.

Because she was currently in a tiny plane, really high up off the ground, strapped to a stranger, about to jump out of the freaking plane.

All because Falcon had pissed her off.

"You don't have to do this," Falcon said, looking rugged, manly, and not at all scared. He was also strapped to an instructor, which was hilarious, but she was too scared to think anything was funny, so not hilarious.

"Seriously?" She looked at him. "If I were strapped to you right now, you'd be encouraging me to do it. And instead you're trying to treat me like I'm small, just because you're not the one protecting me."

He grinned. "Maybe the whole thing was a ploy to get you to jump."

"What?" Disbelief shot through her. "You manipulated me?"

His smile widened. "No, I didn't. I'm not that clever."

"You are that clever. But you're not that mean. You're just too much testosterone."

Ralph leaned over her shoulder. "Five seconds count down."

"Oh, God." She closed her eyes. She didn't want to do this. She didn't want to do this. She was so stupid. She'd decided to jump out of a plane because a man she was paying to protect her had tried to protect her? She was an idiot. A full idiot. "I take it back. You can be overprotective. I'm not going to jump." Wait. Was Ralph still counting down? "Wait, Ralph—"

Suddenly, she was out of the plane, and on her way to her death.

∼

"Holy crap! Oh my God!"

Falcon grinned as Bella leapt to her feet, screaming as Ralph began unhooking her.

"Was it fun?" he asked her.

"That was magical! I jumped out of a plane!" She was jumping up and down as Ralph did his best to unhook her while she was moving. "Did you see the skyline? And the ocean? I saw Nantucket! I freaking saw Nantucket from the air! And the Boston skyline! What the heck, Falcon!"

Falcon got detached from his instructor, thanking him as Bella jumped up and down, still shouting. Her face was glowing. She looked radiant, vibrant, and stunned.

He knew how that felt. He'd never forget his first jump. Absolutely fucking surreal.

Ralph finally got her unstrapped, and she threw her arms around him. "Thank you, Ralph! Oh my God! Thank you for not getting me killed! That was amazing." She hugged him again, and then took off across the grass, sprinting toward Falcon.

He barely had time to brace himself before she flung herself at him. He caught her hips as she wrapped her legs around his waist and hugged him. "Thank you so much, Falcon!"

He grinned as she hugged him. She was so energized, bouncing around, that he had to focus to keep from dropping her. "Feels good, huh?"

She pressed her palms to either side of his face. "Thank you," she whispered. "Thank you for giving me what I didn't know I needed. I appreciate you."

He tightened his grip on her hips as a deep realization struck him.

Bella Hart was his whole world.

She was his everything, and that would never, ever change.

Which meant...yeah.

It did mean that.

FOURTEEN

BELLA GRINNED as Falcon's hands tightened on her hips, holding her up. "Seriously, I was so mad at you, but that was the best thing ever."

He broke out into a grin, a happy, dimpled grin that was so cute she almost started giggling. "Glad I could be helpful."

"Helpful?" She rolled her eyes. "That was amazing."

His smile widened. "Want to go again?"

She grimaced. "God, no. Never again." Her giddiness faded as he stared at her, emotion etched on his handsome face. She realized how good his hands felt on her hips, how close their faces were to each other. All she'd have to do was lean in and—

No. She couldn't kiss him. That would change everything between them. She needed him being her friend, not a man her heart wanted.

But she didn't let go.

And neither did he.

Words faded until it was just them. "I—" She stopped.

"You what?" he asked, his voice rough.

She wasn't okay enough to start anything with him, or anyone. But especially him. She wouldn't mess with him or their relationship. There could be no one-night stand with Falcon. If she crossed that line with him, knowing how he felt about her, knowing how susceptible she was to him, it would be a mistake on so many levels. And cruel, to him, and also to herself. "I can't," she whispered.

"Can't what?"

"Kiss you. Start anything. I'm not there."

He shifted his grip on her hips, not letting her down. "Empty sex maybe? No emotions. No traps. Just raw, sweaty sex?"

She started laughing. "I'm not built for empty sex. Especially not with you."

"Because I'm the man of your dreams."

"You *were* the man of my dreams, back when I dreamed about falling in love." She lowered her legs from his hips, and he released her in a slow, sensual slide down his body. "Now I dream of independence, purpose, and freedom."

He caught her chin as she started to turn away. "Bella—"

She held her breath, her heart racing. If he kissed her, she wouldn't stop him. "What?"

"I'm a grown man. I've been through hell and back a whole ton of times. Don't worry about hurting me. You don't need to protect me from you. If you want this—" He gestured back and forth between them. "—to be something more, and then you decide you need to walk away, I can handle it."

She stared at him, her heart suddenly racing. Had he read her mind? "I would never do that to you."

He raised his brows. "Try it. See if I die."

"Try what?" She paused. "Kissing you?"

He nodded.

She started laughing and put her hands on her hips. "Is this the same approach you used to get me in the airplane? Some sort of warped, reverse psychology?"

"No, I was genuinely planning to ban you from jumping

77

with someone else." He let his hands drop by his sides. "Are you scared to kiss me?"

She swallowed. "Yes."

"Why?"

"Because I might like it too much."

"And then what?"

"I might give up everything to move to the ranch and be your little wife and cook for dude ranch guests for the rest of my life."

"So, you're not scared of me. You're scared of yourself. You don't believe that you will make the choices your soul needs."

Her mouth opened to protest, and then she closed it. He was right. She shrugged, at a loss for words.

He sighed. "Bella, you have survived so much. You chose living on the ranch and cooking for the guests because that is what fit you at that time. If it doesn't fit you, you won't choose it."

She put her hands on her hips. "How do you know?"

"Because I was there the day you showed up under the bridge. I heard how you ended up there. The choices you had to make to protect yourself." He tapped her chest, over her heart. "That courageous girl is still in there. You might have lost sight of her, but she's still in there. That's why you're out in Boston. Because you will never give up on yourself. Ever."

Sudden tears filled her eyes. His faith in her was stunning. His words took her back to her sixteen-year-old self, that awful night when everything changed for her. When she had to grow up so fast.

He kissed her forehead and pulled her in for a hug.

She let herself dissolve into his strength, burying her face in his chest as she wrapped her arms around his waist. She didn't want to cry. She never let herself cry. But it felt so good in his arms, and she felt like she didn't have to be strong anymore. She could just stop trying so hard and lean on him with her whole soul.

He kissed the top of her head and rested his cheek against her hair, still hugging her. Not a sexual overture. More like a giant, armed teddy bear who would never abandon her, never let her forget who she was and what she could accomplish.

She squeezed her eyes shut, breathing in the scent of his body. Woodsy, faint spice, and maybe pine. Familiar. Safe. "I want to stay in your arms forever, but that makes me weak."

"It doesn't make you weak," he said quietly. "Knowing how to fuel yourself for the challenges ahead is critical for success. Sometimes the fuel you need is sleep. Sometimes it's food. Exercise. Meditation. And sometimes, it's simply allowing a moment to let down your guard, connect with someone close to your heart, and let yourself feel safe."

And loved.

She also felt loved.

Not simply loved as part of a big family, but loved all by herself.

She pulled back, lifted her face to his, and then before she could think about it, she slid her hands behind his head, pulled him down toward her, and kissed him.

FIFTEEN

KISSING FALCON WAS MORE amazing than Bella had ever dreamed, and at one time, she'd dreamed about it a lot.

His mouth was intoxicating, his lips softer than she would have imagined. He responded to the kiss instantly, sliding his hand to the nape of her neck, his touch so gentle and tender that she knew she could slide out of his grasp with barely a whisper of movement.

The realization of how free she was to walk away made her lean in closer to him.

He looped his other arm around her back, drawing her against him, so their torsos were touching. Pure heat from his skin melted through her clothes, and energy rippled through her, sparking down her spine to her belly.

God, she wanted more. He was intoxicating, delicious, and everything she'd ever wanted. This man, this amazing man holding onto her as if she was a delicate flower he was protecting, had always been the one she'd wanted.

Falcon.

Falcon.

Falcon.

She didn't even know his last name. Why didn't she know his last name? She pulled back. "How do I not know your last name? After all these years?"

He blinked, clearly trying to recalibrate himself after the sudden question. "I don't have a last name. Just Falcon."

"You don't have a last name? Really?"

He nodded. "You took the name Hart. I didn't want to belong to anyone. So I just dropped my birth name, chose a name for myself, and that was it."

I didn't want to belong to anyone. The words hit deep in her soul. She knew the gut-wrenching loneliness of having absolutely no one, before she'd found Brody and the others. And Falcon had kept them all at a distance over the years. Alone on his quest for vengeance, born when he was just a little boy.

She touched his face. "Falcon," she said softly. "I'm sorry."

He pressed a kiss to her palm. "For what?"

"For all your nights of loneliness."

He stared at her for a long moment, then inclined his head. "I never slowed down long enough to feel lonely. My quest kept me company every minute of every day." He shrugged.

"And now that it's over?"

He inclined his head. "It's fine."

It wasn't fine. She could feel it. "How about we go grab lunch? My treat."

He looked like he was going to say something, but then he simply nodded. "All right." He slung his arm over her shoulder and tucked her against his side in a move that was utterly casual, and at the same time, so protective that it sent heat roaring through her body.

For so long, Falcon had been a fantasy.

Then he'd been a familiar figure who drifted into sight from time to time.

But she realized he'd never been a real human being to her. She'd never seen him as a complex man with a past, a present, and a future that he was trying to unravel.

For the first time in her life, Falcon was real, truly real.

And that made everything so much more complicated, in so many ways.

SIXTEEN

FALCON LEANED BACK, his arm over the deck railing, watching everyone in the restaurant, on the beach, and milling around on the sidewalk and parking lot.

He was feeling very grateful for his highly attuned observation skills, because he could keep an eye on everyone around them, and also be focused on Bella.

Her hair was blowing in the light breeze, and her sunglasses hid her gorgeous blue eyes. She looked relaxed and happy, like a woman without a care in the world.

He knew some of what she hid beneath that smile, but at the same time, he could sense the lightness in her spirit.

Jumping out of the plane had healed something inside her, and he knew it.

"Falcon? What are you thinking?" she asked as she raised her glass of water to take a sip.

He spoke without realizing what he was saying. "That jump healed something inside you. A past trauma, maybe. Or an old identity. I can't tell what it is exactly, but I can tell that it has healed."

She paused, the water glass halfway to her mouth. "What?"

He waved his hand toward her heart. "There's gold in your heart now that wasn't there before. Some of the shadows are gone."

She put her glass down. "Gold? In my heart?"

"Gold light." He moved his fingers in an instinctive design, tracking the shape of the gold he could see in her heart chakra. "It's—" He froze suddenly, his fingers in midair, aware of Bella staring at him like he was crazy.

Son of a bitch. He dropped his hand, picked up his drink, and looked away. "I wonder when our food is going to get here."

Bella leaned forward. "Falcon. What's going on?"

He looked across the beach. "Nothing. I don't see any threats."

She touched his arm, making him jump. "Talk to me, Falcon."

He ground his jaw. Hell, he liked it when she touched him. "No." He knew damn well that any chance he had with Bella would end if she knew the truth about him. "It's nothing." He turned to face her. "Do you have the address to the event tonight? I'd like to drive by after lunch and check it out so I can figure out the best way to keep you safe."

Bella sat back in her chair and folded her arms over her chest. "Well, this will take care of that great kiss. Thanks."

He raised his brows. "What will?"

"You shutting me out. I mean, the kiss was amazing, and I was thinking I wanted to do it again, but then you became an uncommunicative oaf, and it reminded me of why I will never date again, so I appreciate it." She stood up. "In fact, I think I'm going to go do something in a big crowd right now. I'll see you."

He started laughing. "Hell, Bella. You think you're weak?"

She tossed him a look. "No. I jumped out of a plane. Now I think I'm a badass. Honestly, I wouldn't even have cared about your gold light thing, but you got so weird about it that now I want to know."

Falcon clasped his hands behind his head and swore.

Bella sat back down and put her purse on the table.

He studied her.

She waited.

Weirdly, a part of him wanted to tell her what was going on with him. A part of him wanted some help. Someone to tell him he wasn't crazy. But… "I'm fucking terrified that if I tell you, you'll walk away and I'll never see you again. And you'll ban the rest of the Harts from me."

Her eyes widened. "I'd never do that."

He let out his breath. "I have so little to count on, Bella. I can't lose what I have."

She leaned forward, her arms stretched out toward him. "We'll always be there for each other, Falcon. Always. Our past holds us linked."

"The past you want to walk away from?"

She nodded. "Yep, that very past."

He looked past her, staring at the patrons behind her. "I don't know how to trust people," he finally said. But sitting there with Bella, he wanted to. He fucking wanted to build a bridge with her, but he had no idea how.

He looked down at his hands, which had started to burn again. He reached out and took Bella's hand. "Feel hot now?"

As he knew she would, she looked surprised. "Your hand feels like it's on fire. Why?"

He released her hand and flexed his fingers, wanting to haul ass to the ocean and plunge his hands in there. "When I put my hands in salt water, it helps."

She cocked her head, curiosity evident on her face. "Did you contract some tropical disease or something?"

He shrugged. "Something like that." That was all he could say.

She leaned back. "Something like that," she repeated.

He could hear the disappointment in her voice. He'd hurt her by not telling her what was going on. Fuck. He wanted to be a husband and dad. He wanted to give kids a home that he never had. And here he was, with the woman he wanted, shutting her out because he was scared?

Fuck.

Was this what it was like to have a relationship? Because if it was, then…

Then he had to be what she deserved. "Fine." He leaned forward. "When I was in Sedona, Arizona a few years ago, I met this guy and he said, I was a healer."

She blinked. "A healer?"

"Yeah. I met him at a roadside tavern, and he walked up and said I was a healer, and I was blocking it. He said the world needed me, and I was shutting down my gift."

To his surprise, Bella didn't tell him he was crazy. "What kind of healer?" she asked instead.

He shrugged and waved his hands. "Apparently, I have magic hands. I can touch people and heal them. Past traumas, and also physical healing."

Her eyes widened. "Can you?"

"Can I?" He leaned in, surprised by her reaction, as if it could be true. "Don't you think it's weird? And I'm crazy?"

Bella's face softened. "Falcon, the world needs gifts like that. I've never met anyone who can do it, but why wouldn't it be possible? And why not you?"

"Because I grew up in violence, surrounded by drug addiction and murder. And I spent half my life in the darkest of places chasing a vile monster. I'm too tainted and dirty to save anyone."

"Hey." She sat up. "Never say that. None of us are dirt. It doesn't matter what we've done or been through. You know that. How can you even say that? Our circumstances don't devalue our worth. Ever."

He ran his hands through his hair, restless. Unsettled. He wanted to move. To run. "Bella, the things I've done over the last twenty years would make you want to never look at me again—"

"Shut up." She leaned forward. "Can you heal people with your touch, Falcon?"

"No." He threw up his hands, surrendering to her questions. He couldn't make her see the stains on his soul if she didn't want to. It was irritating, but at the same time, he felt like dropping to his knees in gratitude. "No, I can't heal people," he answered. "Ever since he told me that, my hands burn when there's someone near me who needs help. I tried a couple times, and nothing. I can see colors around people sometimes now. Like your heart. Weird shit happens around me. To me. I think I'm going crazy. And yeah, so yeah. I just —" He held up his hands. "They fucking burn. And I see colors. And I know things. And that's…yeah. I talk to spirit guides, but they haven't helped me with this healing thing. And—" He cut himself off. "So, yeah."

Fuck. He felt uncomfortable. Life was so much easier when he ate every meal alone.

Bella held out her hands. "Falcon."

"I don't need sympathy. I just—" He looked at her, suddenly desperate. "Am I fucking crazy, Bella? You'd tell me the truth, right? Sometimes I think I could heal someone, but it's just out of my reach. Am I…crazy?"

"No," she said. "Take my hands, Falcon."

He shifted, but he put his hands in hers.

She tightened her grip on him. "Falcon, when people go through really hard things, they become more. We've all experienced it. I think it makes perfect sense that a man like you would become a bright, shining light after darkness tried to drown him."

He looked down at her hands around his. She was holding onto him. Not pushing him away. Not rejecting him. Holding onto him. "I can't do it, though. If it is a gift I have, then I'm not worthy enough to have it."

She squeezed his hands. "Oh, Falcon," she whispered. "That's the lie everyone tells themselves. That we're not worthy of what we want, of what we dream of, of who we are meant to be, of life at the highest level. But it's not true. We're all worth it."

He closed his eyes, focusing on the feel of her hands in his. "If I was, then I'd be able to do it."

"Really?"

He opened his eyes. "Yeah."

"Or is it possible you just don't know how to do it? That no one taught you? That you have to learn how to do it like anything else in life? Or that you've decided you can't, so you're blocking it? Are any of those options possible? Is it remotely possible that there's another reason why you don't heal people, other than that you aren't worthy of it?"

He stared at her, contemplating her response. "I don't know," he said slowly.

"Of course you don't know. Because who knows how that works? I don't know."

Laughter started bubbling up inside him. "That's a lot of 'knows' happening there."

She threw up her hands. "I know!"

They both burst out laughing, and suddenly his tension was gone. Simply *gone*. After years of thinking he was losing his mind, Bella had made him feel normal. Safe.

Safe.

He sat back, stunned by the word that had popped into his mind. Safe. He never thought about being safe or not. He just got up every day and lived it. But until this moment, this healer shit had scared him.

And suddenly, it didn't.

SEVENTEEN

BEFORE FALCON HAD a chance to relax, Bella tapped his palm. "Who is making your hands heat up right now? Who needs you?"

He tensed. "I don't know. There are a lot of people around."

Bella raised her brows. "Look around. See."

"Bella—"

She leaned forward. "If you really can heal people, and you're refusing to do it, then you're betraying yourself, the world, and everyone who was like us as kids, needing help, with nowhere to turn. If you can help one person avoid the kind of suffering we both lived with, and you refuse to even try, how can you live with that?"

He stared at her, anger rising from deep inside of him. "I've fucking spent my life trying to make a difference."

"No. You spent your life on a revenge quest, which is now over, and *now* you get the chance to maybe be to someone what Brody was to us. Safety. Love. A chance at life."

He fisted his hands. "I'm not that man."

"Maybe not." She tapped his balled-up hand. "Look around. Tell me who it is. You know that. I know you do."

He stared at her. "Bella—"

"Is it her?" She pointed at a woman walking past on the boardwalk.

He couldn't keep himself from glancing over. "No."

"What about that man on the beach with the red towel?"

His gaze slid out across the sand. "No."

"The little girl in the yellow hat putting sunscreen on her legs?"

Unable to stop himself, he sought out the yellow hat girl on the beach. She was sitting with what appeared to be her parents and sister. "No—" He paused as his gaze went behind the family to a boy with brown skin. He was alone, building a sandcastle. Maybe seven years old.

The moment he saw the boy, he knew. "Fuck."

"Him?" Bella followed his gaze. "He looks fine."

"He's not." Falcon's hands were on fucking fire.

"Let's go talk to him." She pushed back her seat, but he grabbed her arm.

"Any man who walks up to a kid on a beach and starts talking to him is going to get arrested," he said. "Especially one who looks like me."

"Tall, dark, and handsome?"

"Ragged, haunted, and big."

Her face softened. "I see beauty when I look at you, Falcon."

Something turned over at her words, and suddenly all he wanted to do was sweep her up in his arms and get out of there with her. "I'm glad to hear that, Bella, but that's not how that kid's mom will see me."

Bella looked at him, then sighed. "You're right. And you're burning my arm."

He released her. "Sorry." He pulled out his wallet. "I'm done here. Let's hit the road—"

"However, I'm an adorable woman. I won't get arrested."

She moved fast, ducking out of his reach before he realized she was moving.

He swore. "Bella—"

But she was already gone, hopping over the deck railing and landing on the boardwalk, like a woman who lived on a ranch and was used to climbing fences all day. He swore as she ran over to a little cart of beach gear, bought a set of toys, and a towel, and then headed across the sand.

He almost started laughing as she spread out the towel a few feet from the boy, sat down, and pulled out her sand-castle building equipment. He leaned back in his seat, folding his arms across his chest as he watched her hurry to the shore with a big bucket, fill it, and then return, carrying that bucket as if it were nothing.

She sat down on her towel and started building, not even looking at the boy, but the boy was watching her. It took only a minute for Bella to start chatting with the boy, and another minute or two after that until the boy was beside her, and they were building a sandcastle together.

The sight of Bella and the little boy made something inside Falcon tighten. She was so beautiful with the little boy. A natural. She knew how to make kids feel at ease, because she, like the rest of the Harts, knew how fucking painful childhood could be. Like the others, she wanted to do whatever she could to help other at-risk kids avoid what they experienced.

She would make such a difference to kids, if she decided to be a mom.

He respected that she didn't want to be, but hell, she was beautiful to watch with the boy.

As he watched her, Falcon became aware of a man nearby who was also watching Bella. Too closely. He bolted upright, his adrenaline igniting. A random admirer, or danger?

He couldn't tell.

Swearing, he tossed cash on the table, then followed

Bella's path over the railing. The minute his feet hit the ground, he was in motion, sprinting across the boardwalk and the beach until he was beside the man, just behind his right shoulder.

The man didn't notice him, so caught up in watching Bella.

Falcon's hands were tingling, and his entire body was coiled for action.

He saw Bella look up. Her gaze went back and forth between Falcon and the man. Then understanding dawned. She immediately moved, putting herself between the man and the boy.

Son of a bitch. That was his job to move into the line of fire. Not hers.

He took a breath, opened his senses, and then put his hand on the man's shoulder. The instant he made contact, the man's energy hit him hard. It was a lot of crap, but nowhere in there was an intent to harm.

The man spun toward him, a look of surprise on his face. "What?"

Falcon pulled his hand back. "Nothing. My mistake."

He wanted to claim Bella as his woman, but he knew she wouldn't like that. Just as how he had wanted to belong to no one back when he was younger, Bella would never want to be claimed by a man.

But he did decide to go over and sit with her.

Because she'd want him to. Not to be a possessive male or anything like that.

Or to be exactly that.

He strode past the man, and then crouched down beside Bella. "The man is fine," he said softly. "No problem with him."

Bella relaxed and flashed him a smile. "Great." She immediately moved aside. "Gordy, this is my friend Falcon. Can he build with us?"

Gordy glanced at Falcon, and the minute Falcon locked eyes with the boy, he couldn't breathe. Extreme fear, pain, and sadness slammed him, locking up his lungs and freezing him in place.

It was the boy's pain, not his, and Falcon could feel it in every cell of his body.

He felt like he was Gordy, a seven-year-old kid carrying more pain than any human should ever have, let alone a kid.

His hands burned like an inferno, and he shoved them into the bucket of seawater.

Bella frowned. "Are you okay, Falcon?"

He took a breath, trying to center himself. He'd never felt such an extreme reaction to someone before, one which enabled him to feel their pain so intensely. His extremities felt cold, but he could feel the heat in his hands. He felt shaky and weak.

What. The. Hell.

"Shake his hand," Bella whispered. "Introduce yourself."

No way was he touching Gordy. He'd fry the kid's hand right off. Instead, he shot the kid a smile that he hoped was friendly, because he didn't have a lot of experience trying to make kids feel at ease. "Yeah, I'm Falcon."

Gordy stared at him. "Are you a monster?"

A monster. A fucking *monster*. Why yes, yes he was.

Bella's eyes widened and she hit Falcon's thigh. "Falcon just got back from the jungle. He's an adventurer. He didn't take a bath for three months."

Falcon almost started laughing at the surprise on Gordy's face. "Three months?"

"Yeah, when you're a grown up, you can do that." His hands were burning so much he felt like they were going to catch fire. "Good to meet you, Gordy, but Bella and I need to go."

"What? No." Bella sat more firmly in the sand. "Gordy, how are you feeling? Okay?"

Gordy's gaze swiveled to Bella. "Fine."

"Are you? Really?" she pressed.

Falcon saw Gordy's confused look, and he swore under his breath. "Bella, let it go."

"But you said—"

"I know what I said, but that's not how this works."

"You don't know how it works," she snapped. "Gordy, Falcon is---"

"Leaving." Falcon stood up and dragged Bella to her feet. "Let's go."

She pulled her arm away from him. "You don't get to tell me—"

"This is my life, Bella. Not yours. You don't get to run it for me." He kept his voice low, but he couldn't keep the edge out of his voice. "And Gordy's life belongs to him. He's too young to give me permission even if I could help him, which I can't."

Bella scowled at him. "You have a gift—"

"No. Some guy in Arizona told me I have a gift. It's not the same thing." And to think he'd been afraid Bella would think he was crazy. He clearly should have been prepared for the opposite reaction.

"How would you know—"

"Gordy!" A woman hurried up. "I'm so sorry if he's bothering you. Gordy, you're supposed to stay with the group."

Falcon shoved Bella behind him and moved his body between the woman and Bella. "He's not bothering us," Falcon said.

Bella leaned around him. "He was helping me build my sandcastle."

"He's supposed to stay with the group. I can't keep track of them if they run off." The woman took Gordy's hand. "Come on, honey. Let's go back with the others."

She smiled at Falcon and Bella, and then headed off with Gordy. Falcon watched as the woman took him toward a group of eleven kids. They were all wearing matching turquoise tee shirts, he realized. "Field trip?"

"Maybe." Bella stood beside him, watching as closely as he was.

Because they both had the same instinct. "Foster kids?" he asked finally.

"Or underprivileged kids," Bella said. "I can feel it. Can't you? They're like us. Like we were."

"Yeah, they are." He wanted to go ask questions. He wanted to find out more. But today wasn't about those kids. Today was about keeping Bella alive.

The kids would have to wait.

"Do you want to go over there and talk to them?" Bella asked.

Yes. But no. If Gordy thought he was a monster, so would the others. There was no way he was throwing more trauma in their direction. "Nope. I'm good." He quickly surveyed the beach to see if there were any threats, saw about a hundred people who were all within shooting range of Bella, and decided to get them the hell off the sand. "Let's go. Back to the house."

"To the house?" She frowned at him. "But—"

"Did you forget that someone was hunting you last night?"

She blinked. "Hunting me?"

"Yeah." He put his hand on her lower back and guided her toward the boardwalk.

She looked over at him. "Your hand is burning my back."

"I know."

"Don't you want to help Gordy?"

"He thinks I'm a monster."

Her face softened. "You're not a monster."

"No?" He was rethinking fast and hard his desire to be a foster parent. If Gordy had thought he was a monster, would he be doing more harm than good if he tossed his scarred ass into the lives of traumatized kids?

Fuck. He would, wouldn't he? He looked back over at the group of kids Gordy was with and his jaw hardened. Those kids need something he couldn't provide them: a feeling of being safe.

They *would* be safe with him, but if they didn't believe it...

And maybe they wouldn't be safe with him.

Maybe they'd become hunted just like Bella.

Which meant he wasn't good for any of them.

For anyone.

EIGHTEEN

BELLA LEANED on the counter at her cottage, watching Falcon as he stalked around the living room, checking out the windows, inspecting the ocean like he expected Jaws to rise up out of it, and being entirely uncommunicative.

She sighed as she watched him.

One kiss, and she'd fallen hard for him.

The kiss had been magical, everything she'd always dreamed she deserved.

And then everything had gotten all twisted.

He'd become cranky and withdrawn. Restless. Tense.

Shutting her out.

He'd been like that ever since he'd told her about the healing gift, and it had gotten worse since the incident with Gordy.

When she'd asked, he'd said he was focusing on keeping her safe.

Which was silly because she could keep herself safe. She'd hired him to keep Brody from abducting her, but having Falcon keep her locked in her cottage might be even less fun than being trapped on the ranch.

She deserved more than this.

She hadn't stayed single for this long to fall for a man who gave her the opposite of her freedom and a feeling of connection. "Falcon?"

He was currently peering out the side window, toward the house next door. "Yeah?"

"Could you tell what was wrong with Gordy?" One last attempt. She was giving him one last chance to be the guy she wanted.

He was silent.

She ground her jaw in frustration. "Damn you, Falcon."

He looked over at her, surprise on his face. "What?"

"*What?* You have to *ask* what?"

His brow furrowed. "Apparently. What's wrong?"

"You." She stalked over to him and poked him in the chest. "You give me this amazing kiss that makes me want to fall for you, and then you immediately start on this spiraling descent into silence, distance, and shutting me out. For your information, any chance you had with me is officially over, and you proved to me why I'm going to go get some cats to sleep with because men just aren't worth it."

Pain flickered across his face, pain so raw and stark she caught her breath. "Makes sense," he said. "Probably a smart choice. I'm going to check out back."

Then he walked past her.

He literally dismissed her.

"Are you kidding?" She grabbed a pillow and threw it at him. It hit him in the back of the head, and he spun around to face her, looking startled. "Yes, I still remember how to throw things at you, you big jerk."

He stared at her, then tossed the pillow on the couch and started walking toward the back door.

What the heck was wrong with him?

He was back to being the silent shadow that had drifted in and out of her life for so many years, only this time, he didn't have the excuse of being on some obsessive quest.

"No!" She shouted at him. "You don't get to treat me like that!"

He spun around to face her. "Like what?"

"Like I don't matter." She put her hands on her hips. "I was there the night you literally crawled into our encampment, covered in blood. Blood, Falcon. *Blood!* I heard you and Brody arguing about taking you to the hospital. You were *dying* and you were so worried about being caught by the cops that you were willing to die first."

His face became impassive. "You were there that night?"

"Yes. We were all there!" She threw up her hands. "Why do you not let yourself connect with me? Where is that emotion I saw for a second?"

He ground his jaw. "My focus is to keep you safe—"

"Do you remember the night we met?"

He blinked. "Of course."

"Because I do. I had just been chased fourteen blocks by a group of boys. I thought I was going to die that night. A teenage girl living on the streets is going to get attacked by a guy at some point. It's just a matter of time."

He stared at her.

"I thought my time had come. I got to our encampment, and no one was there. I couldn't run anymore, and the boys were right behind me. I collapsed to my knees, crawled into one of the sleeping bags, and hoped they wouldn't see I was in there. I didn't pray, because I didn't believe anymore." Her chest started to ache as she remembered that night. "They'd thrown bottles at me, and I was cut and bleeding. I'd fallen twice and my hands were bleeding."

He swore under his breath, but he was watching her intently now.

"I crawled into that sleeping bag and tried to hold my breath, but I was panting. I couldn't be quiet. I heard them come in, and one of them said I was in the sleeping bag. I hadn't let myself cry in years, but when I heard him say that, I started crying. I wished I had died instead of having to endure what was coming."

He swore under his breath. "Bella, you don't need to relive that—"

She lifted her chin. "I felt one of them grab the sleeping bag, but before he could pull it, he screamed. I heard the thud of his body hitting the side of the bridge. I thought Brody had come back, so I scrambled out of the sleeping bag in time to see this guy I'd never met taking down this entire group of boys. He scared them so badly I could hear them screaming for blocks as they ran away. I knew they'd never come back, and they'd never come near me again, because this danger-ous, terrifying man had told them that I was under his protec-tion and if anything ever happened to me, he would find them and hurt them in ways that would make them wish for the death that would never come."

A small smile quirked the corner of his mouth. "If they lived in terror for the rest of their lives, I feel like that's fair."

She looked at him. "And then this guy turned to me, and said, 'You must be Bella. I'm a friend of Brody's. My name's Falcon, and I'll protect you.'" Tears filled her eyes as she recalled that moment. "It was the first time in a decade that I felt safe," she whispered. "You got the medical kit, and you told me stories as you fixed me up. You made me laugh, when I thought I'd never laugh again. You made me believe in heroes, in good people, and in hope."

Emotion flickered over Falcon's face. "I did?"

"You did. For the rest of my life, that has been the defining moment that has kept my heart open."

He ran his hand through his hair. "I—I didn't know. I was just trying to do the right thing."

"Because that's what you do. You are light. You are love. Even when you live in darkness. Do you remember how you taught me self-defense every time you saw me? Making me strong. Teaching me so that I'd never be scared again."

He nodded. "I remember. You were hungry to learn."

"I wanted to be the one to protect others like you did for me." She lifted her chin. "And instead, I've been hiding on a ranch for years."

He walked over to her. "No. You're not hiding. You've been healing."

She lifted her chin as he approached. "You were kind to me, Falcon. On the outside, you were huge, strong, and dirty. But you had this amazing gentleness that made me feel like there was kindness in the world. Like a badass teddy bear."

He slid his hand behind her neck, his touch warm, soothing, safe. God, she loved it when he touched her. "That night, I was leaving camp when I saw you run up. I'd told Brody I wasn't sticking around, and I didn't want to get entangled with a makeshift family of homeless kids. I had no intention of getting involved, until I saw you running for your life, torn jeans, no shoes, your face absolutely rocked with terror."

She lifted her chin, intentionally separating herself from the shadows of the emotions she'd felt that night. "I thought I was going to die. And I might have."

"The minute I saw you, my world as I knew it came to a screaming halt. I was already on the move to protect you when you dove into that sleeping bag. I threw that kid like he was nothing, and I thought I killed him when he hit the bridge." He placed his other hand on the other side of her face, cupping her in his grasp. "I had never killed anyone before, but when he hit, I hoped he was dead, and that scared the crap out of me. I would have run at that point, but I was afraid they'd come back."

She smiled. "My protector."

"I followed you for a month. Everywhere you went, I followed you."

She blinked. "You did?"

"Yeah. I had to make sure I'd scared them. A couple times, you passed one of them, and I made sure they saw me. Eventually, when you walked by, they just took off and ran the other way. I knew they'd never bother you again." He let out his breath, his voice soft and rough. "You were the only light I'd ever had in my life, Bella. I would do anything to keep you safe."

"Including walk away from me."

He nodded. "Yeah."

She looped her fingers around his wrists. "Including shutting me out today?"

His eyes darkened, and he didn't answer.

In the silence that fell between them, she felt her heart begin to shatter, piece by piece. She'd tried everything to reach him, and she'd failed. "Never mind—"

He didn't release her. "Gordy saw a monster when he looked at me today," he said quietly.

Her gaze snapped to his. "I know."

"He saw me through the lens of his trauma. I thought I could help kids like Gordy because I'd been through what they're going through, but I just scared him."

Bella heard the pain in his voice, and her heart softened. "He asked if you were a monster. He didn't say you were scary."

Falcon blinked. "What?"

"You were like a monster coming out of the shadows the night we met, but you were *my* monster, and that made me safe. Sometimes, we need monsters to protect us, because regular humans aren't enough."

Falcon stared at her, and she could see the doubt in his eyes. He didn't believe he was good. He didn't believe he could make the difference he wanted to make. "If I brought a kid into my life, it could make him a target, like it did with you. So I can't keep him safe. I'll put him in danger."

Bella put her hands on either side of Falcon's face, mimicking his pose with her. "You don't know that my stalkers are related to your quest. But even if they are, it's worth it because of what you give me."

He cocked his brow. "What do I give you?"

"When you shut me out? Heartbreak. Pain. Loneliness." When he started to pull away, she tightened her grip. "But when you look at me like you are doing right now, when you listen to me, when you talk to me about the things that matter to you, you become the beautiful man who makes me want to fall into your arms and never leave them."

Her declaration hung in the air between them. Her heart was racing. She knew there was so much past between them, and so much space between them now, but in this moment, it didn't matter. This was Falcon. Hero. Protector. A man with a heart shining bright with goodness and beauty, even if he fought so hard not to let it show.

He moved closer, sliding his fingers through her hair. "I don't know what to do right now." His voice was low, rough.

"What do you mean?" *Kiss me, Falcon. Just kiss me.*

He searched her face. "I cause you pain. I'm trying to be different, but I'm not good at it. I'm danger. I'll probably fuck up every future dream you have. I—"

"Do you want to kiss me?"

He met her gaze. "More than anything I've wanted in my life."

"Then do it."

He didn't move, and her heart sank. He was going to make her kiss him first, wasn't he? As he'd promised? She loved that he kept his promise, but underneath all her bravado, she still wanted a knight in shining armor to sweep her off her feet.

"Bella." He whispered her name, so reverently that she felt tears well in her eyes.

"No one has ever said my name like that," she whispered.

"Because no one has ever loved you like I do." Then he angled his head, leaned down, and kissed her.

NINETEEN

FALCON HAD WAITED years for this moment. A lifetime...and beyond...to be able to lean down, pull this incredible woman into his arms, and kiss her like she was the light that carried the entire world in its rays.

But the moment he felt Bella's mouth against his, he knew that he'd fully underestimated the impact it would have on his soul.

Her lips were warm, soft, perfection, magical luminaries that poured wholeness into the very depths of his being.

He'd meant to kiss her once and let her go, but when she kissed him back, there was no chance of him pulling away. And when she slid her arms around his neck and pulled him against her, he knew that he was lost to her. He always had been.

"Bella," he whispered her name as he trailed his lips down the side of her neck, almost unable to believe he was there with her. Her skin was slightly salty from the hot day, and he loved it.

He kissed over her collarbone and her throat, then caught her face between his palms and kissed her again. More. Deeper. Fighting desperately for the class and patience she

104

deserved. But he'd been thinking about this moment for so long, he had to fight to stay in control, to give her long, leisurely, tantalizing kisses that tasted like heaven.

On second thought, those kisses were exactly what he needed.

He leaned into them, letting them slow his pace, bring him into the present, into this insane moment with Bella. He had no idea how this was happening, and he was pretty sure it shouldn't be, but he had no chance to play the hero and step back when she was holding onto him so tightly.

With every kiss, he made sure he paid close attention to her body language, prepared to pull back if she gave any indication she didn't want what was happening between them.

But she didn't. She leaned into him, kissing him back, even taking the kiss to the next level. And the one after that, until he felt like he was on fire, burning for her. "Couch?" he murmured against her mouth.

"Bed."

Oh, fuck. He pulled back then, breathing hard as he searched her face. "You're sure?"

"I don't know what I'm sure of, but let's start there and see." She paused. "I assume you can stop yourself at any point? I'm not promising anything by saying bed—"

He laughed and swept her up in his arms, cradling her against his chest. "You're always safe with me, Bella. On that, I will stake my life."

She giggled and looped her arm around his neck as he made his way across the small cottage. "I know I'm safe with you. Every girl needs a man who makes her feel completely and wholly safe."

"Every woman deserves that." He stepped into the bedroom, broke the kiss long enough to take one more look around the cottage, then kicked the door shut and locked it.

He lowered Bella gently to the bed, careful not to jostle

her, but the minute she landed on the comforter, she grabbed him and yanked him off balance. He let her tug him over, and he landed beside her. He rolled onto his back and pulled her on top of him.

She came willingly, bracing her hands on either side of his head as she leaned over him and kissed him, her knees on either side of his hips.

He grinned at the twinkle in her eye, and some of his tension eased. "You're happy right now." He had his hands on her hips, drawing circles with his thumbs. He loved having her sitting on him. It put her in the position of power, which he wanted to give her. It also meant that she wanted to be there, because it would be so easy for her to get off.

"I am." She giggled. "Why am I happy? I don't know. Maybe because this super-hot guy I've had a crush on forever is in my bed?"

"Super-hot?" He laughed softly as he ran his right hand over her thigh. "I'm like a homeless dog. Underfed. Kind of feral."

"Exactly how I want you." She leaned down and kissed him, her breasts grazing his chest.

"Fuck," he whispered. "I don't even know how to handle this. It's you. I'm kissing *you*."

She pulled back. "When you say things like that, in that mushy tone, you make up for all the moments of stony silence you give me."

"I don't want to give you stony silence," he said. "I just... I'm learning. It's hard."

"I know." She put her hands on his shoulders. "I have a question for you, Falcon."

He smiled at her playful tone. "Lay it on me, beautiful."

"Did you ever wish you hadn't turned me down when I asked you to make love to me?"

"No. Never." He laughed at the flash of disappointment on her face. "Sweetheart. I was twenty. You were sixteen and traumatized. There wasn't a chance in hell I was going to cross that line with you until you were ready. Until it would be beautiful and equal and magical for you."

Her face softened. "You deserve magic, too."

"Being with you would always have been magic." He slid his hand beneath her hair on the back of her neck. "But it wouldn't have been magical for you until you were ready." He paused. "What do you think?"

"Am I ready?"

He nodded.

She smiled. "I don't think I could ever be fully ready for you, Falcon, but magical? Oh, yes." Then she lowered herself on top of him and kissed him like she would never let him go.

He surrendered to her, fully, completely, and without hesitation.

TWENTY

BELLA KNEW the minute Falcon committed to what was happening between them.

His kisses took on a new level of heat. His hands came alive, skimming over her body like he would never be able to touch her enough. His mouth took control, and she gave it over to him.

His fingers played around the hem of her shirt, testing, but not making a move. His cautiousness made her smile. She paused and pulled back. "Falcon. I need to have a word with you."

His gaze was sharp and attentive. "What's up?"

She took a breath. "Last night, at the wedding, one of my friends, I'm guessing Tori, put a multipack of condoms in my purse after they all agreed you were smoking hot and there for me. I found them this morning, and I put them in my nightstand."

His fingers tightened on her hip and his gaze shot to the little white table to his left. "Is that so?"

"Yes. There are three different colors. Blue. Yellow. Green."

A slow smile began to play at the corners of his mouth. "I look good in blue."

She giggled. "I was thinking the same thing this morning. It really brings out your eyes."

"My brown eyes?"

"Exactly." She paused, her heart starting to race. Could she do this? Yes. Should she? Probably not. Did she want to do it anyway? She paused to listen to her inner voice. *Yes.*

All right. Future be damned. This was her moment. She could be dead tomorrow. Why not live tonight?

Before she could think about it, she grabbed the hem of her shirt and yanked it over her head. Her pink sports bra wasn't exactly sexy, but the look on his face made her feel like the most gorgeous woman who had ever graced the earth.

"God, you're beautiful," he whispered, tracing his fingers over her ribs, as if he were afraid she was so fragile he could break her.

She smiled. "Thanks." She grabbed the hem of his shirt and gave a light tug, raising her brows in question.

"Hell, yeah." He sat up, pulled his shirt off, and tossed it aside, revealing a chiseled, lean torso with a six pack, a farmer's tan, and more than a few scars. He was so tough, raw, and sexy. Everything she'd imagined, and a thousand times more.

He didn't lie back down. Instead, using those delicious abs, he slid his hands around her waist and drew her in for a kiss that was made so much more intense by the fact that his bare chest was against her now, creating an intimacy they'd never before had.

She leaned against him, wrapping her arms around his neck and settling deeper in his lap as she locked her legs around his waist.

The kiss soon became hotter, his hands bolder, his mouth naughtier, until he finally got daring enough to toss her bra aside and showcase his talents on her breasts. It had been a long time since she'd had any kind of man action, and Falcon unleashed new waves of need and desire she'd never let herself feel before.

Was it because she felt safe with him? Was it because of years of longing? Was it because he was a rebel and a loner, and that appealed to the side of her that was trying to get away from her life and her identity? Or simply because he was who he was, and he was the one for her?

She had no answers, but when both their pants hit the floor, she decided it didn't matter.

This moment with Falcon was perfection, and all she wanted was for her silly mind to take a break and let her experience the magic of Falcon's lovemaking.

His body was hot and muscular, and his palms were rough and insanely tender as he palmed her belly, inviting her to be still while his mouth created sensations she hadn't realized could happen in real life.

She slid her fingers through his hair, needing to ground herself in him as the desire coiled tighter and tighter. He looked up, caught her hand, and pressed a kiss to her finger-tips. "You okay?"

She nodded, her throat suddenly tight.

He frowned and moved up her body, settling his hips on hers. "Tears?" He brushed his finger over her cheek, and she realized she was crying. "Talk to me, sweetheart."

She wiped the back of her hand over her cheek, and it came away wet. "I don't know why I'm crying. I just…" She paused. "It's a lot to be here with you. How you make me feel."

He continued to frown. "I feel like the fact I make you cry isn't a good thing."

"No, it is." She laughed through her tears. "I've never felt like this before. It's…" She paused trying to find the words, but there were none strong enough to describe it. Finally, she put his hand over her heart. "I feel it in here, and it feels amazing."

He smiled then, a slow, beautiful smile that spread across his face into his eyes. "Me, too."

Her heart did a little leap. "Is it bad to admit that I really want you to make love to me?"

"Bad?" A wicked gleam came into his eyes. "You want bad?"

Her belly clenched. "Is there a Bad Falcon?"

"Every part of me is bad."

"It's not."

He laughed. "I know. I also know you know. And no, it's not bad to admit it. It's fantastic, because I feel the same way."

Her heart started racing. "You want it. And I want it. And you look good in blue---"

"I also look good in yellow and green."

"Maybe we should try them all."

"I think we should." Without moving off her, he reached for the nightstand, flipped the drawer open, and pulled out a condom. "Green first?"

"I love green." She felt like she was already out of breath, and she shifted restlessly, wanting more, needing more. Needing what he gave her: freedom, passion, safety, fantasy fulfillment...pure, unconstrained heat.

Falcon made quick work of the condom, but before she had time to get nervous, he apparently decided to make very, very sure she was ready, oh, so ready.

She tipped her head back, gasping as he made his way down her body, taking advantage of every curve, every crevice, every nerve in her body. Within moments, she was completely lost to him. "Falcon," she whispered. "I want you."

"And I want you, my beautiful Bella." He moved back up her, and met her gaze as he slipped inside her. She felt like she was falling into his soul, tumbling freely, in full surrender, trusting him to catch her without fail, no matter how many times she fell.

Then he began to move, and she forgot about everything except fully surrendering, letting go of all her protections, and just trusting.

For what felt like a whisper in time and also forever, sensations flooded her, stripping her of all but the deepest core of her humanity, and then the orgasm took her, sweeping her off the cliff and catapulting her through the air, while he held her safely in his arms, protecting her the whole way down.

Falcon buried his face in Bella's hair, watching the setting sun peeking through the corners of the blinds, holding her close while she slept.

All afternoon with her.

Complete surrender.

Full trust.

Laughter.

Fun.

Passion.

Connection.

It was that last one that was still vibrating deep inside him. *Connection.* There were times that he had felt like one with Bella. He'd felt fully safe with her, and he'd never felt safe in his life.

Not because she would shoot anyone who came for them, but because she held his soul with the greatest of care, and he knew it would always be safe in her hands.

He breathed deeply, inhaling the flowery scent of her hair as he draped his leg over her hips.

Being with Bella had been so much more than he ever could have guessed.

She was his whole world. Worth waiting all this time.

But what did the future hold? She didn't want to get married. Have kids. Move back to the ranch. She didn't even want a relationship.

Would he give up all the things he wanted for a sliver of the light that she was willing to give him?

Right now, he felt no doubt. Absolutely. Without hesitation.

But he also knew that he would always regret not having a family. A wife. Kids. A home.

Would that regret be fair to her? To him?

Maybe he was lying to himself that he could handle a family. Maybe she was right. Maybe this was the path he was supposed to be on.

And then he thought of Gordy, and the other kids in his group. The kids who had no home, like him. Who never would have a home, unless he made one for them.

He pulled back to look at Bella, sleeping in his arms. *Bella.* He loved her. Always had. With all the capability of what was left of his heart. Was it enough? And, enough for what, exactly?

TWENTY-ONE

OH, boy.

Falcon was temptation, so much more than Bella had any business challenging herself with.

They'd been at the catering event for an hour, and Falcon had been circling her, on high alert, watching the crowd, completely standing out among the throngs of well-dressed people. He was wearing jeans, boots, and a light jacket that covered his gun. He looked like a bodyguard.

There was nothing soft or approachable about him.

She was pretty sure everyone there would believe he had spent some time as an assassin for the military or something comparable.

He was hard. He was cold. He was focused.

But after today, she knew the soft side of him, and it was too much to handle, honestly.

He made her want to give up her dreams to be with him, and that would destroy her.

"Bella!"

She turned as Piper and Kitty walked up, grinning with relief to have some girl energy near her. Tears filled her eyes when she saw them. "Hey, guys."

"Whoa!" Kitty put her hands on her hips. "What's with the tears?"

"I'm not crying. I don't cry." Bella wiped her cheeks. "It's all the onions."

"For all that's beautiful and girly, don't lie to me, Bella," Kitty said. "What is going on?"

"I just—" Involuntarily, Bella's gaze went to Falcon, who was still making his rounds, always nearby, but also, always watching everyone in the crowd.

Piper and Kitty followed her gaze, then Piper grinned. "You slept with him?"

Bella lifted her chin. "No, I—"

Kitty snorted. "Another lie! Girl, I'm going to have to retract my recommendation for you to buy Diana's business! I don't like lies!"

Piper frowned at Bella, ignoring her business partner. "What's going on?"

Bella hesitated, but these were the women she wanted to be friends with. This was the life she wanted to build in Boston. "I'm falling for him, but he wants to get married, have kids, and live on the Hart Ranch. I need to get off the ranch, find my own identity, and I don't want to get married or have kids." She paused. "But I feel like I would walk away from everything that matters to me for him."

Understanding filled Piper's face. "The curse of being a woman," she said softly. "All we ever read are stories where women do that."

Kitty looked over at Falcon, and Bella braced herself for more sass.

But Kitty surprised her.

"Bella," Kitty said. "You came out here for you. It's too soon for you to go back."

Bella bit her lip. "I know—"

"If he's right for you, he'll wait."

"He doesn't want to wait. He wants a family." She paused.

"He *needs* a family. And I don't want kids. I just...I don't. I never have. I mean, I didn't before. Not that I do now. I don't." She stopped, confusing herself.

Piper frowned. "Are you saying you'd have kids for him?"

Oh, God. Was she saying that? "I don't know, but going back to the ranch..." She sighed. "I've had a crush on him since I was sixteen. I don't know if that's what's driving my emotions right now. Or if he's just the right guy for me, even today."

Kitty put her hands on her hips. "I'll tell you something, Bella. I met my husband at the peak of my pop star career. I told him I wasn't going to give up my career any time soon, and he said that was fine. But it wasn't. Our marriage couldn't survive my travel. When we had kids, I had to choose to reduce my travel, because at the end of the day, it's the woman who usually has the responsibility for the kids and family."

Piper raised her hand. "That's not how it has to be."

"No, but that's how it is." Kitty held out her hands. "I love my kids. I have never regretted all the love I gave them, but does a part of me regret not giving *myself* the love I needed and wanted? Yes." She touched Bella's shoulder. "You need to love yourself first, sweetheart. Take time to do that. Maybe eventually you'll decide you want kids and a family, and if Falcon's the right guy, he'll be around. But maybe you won't, and then he's not the right guy."

"Unless he changes his mind," Piper said. "He might decide he doesn't want kids and to get married."

Bella thought about how he'd looked at Gordy and the other kids. "It's in his soul to protect kids. He needs it." She knew why he needed it: to erase the darkness that coated his past, to find a way to believe he had worth.

Kitty cocked her head. "Do you think there's any chance you would ever want to get married or have kids?"

Bella shook her head. "It feels like a trap. I've been trapped for so long."

Piper raised her hand. "I need to speak up here. I was very anti-dating, let alone marriage, but with the right guy, it isn't a trap. It's liberating. It's like having your own secret weapon in life."

Bella pressed her lips together. She knew that Piper had had a tough past, and she'd been very opposed to dating, let alone settling down and getting married. She also knew that magic had happened with Piper and Declan. She sighed as she looked over at Falcon.

He was leaning against a pillar nearby, arms folded, scanning the room.

He seemed to sense her looking at him, because his gaze swiveled toward her. His face softened, and he smiled, a smile that went right to her heart. *God, she wanted him.*

Piper put her arm around Bella's shoulders. "The way he looks at you is how Declan looks at me."

"He sure does," Kitty said. "Damn, girl. You've got yourself entangled already. Why even question it? Dive in and see where the ride takes you."

"I agree," Piper said. "Go have fun. If it works out, it's worth it."

Bella thought about getting on a plane with Falcon, walking away from these women, from Boston, from her independence, to move back to the ranch she'd lived on for so long. To cooking for dude ranch guests. To being the same as she always had been. "I'm more than who I've let myself be," she whispered.

"We all are," Kitty agreed.

Bella pulled her shoulders back. "I'm going to buy the catering business."

Piper and Kitty raised their brows. "Are you doing that just to give you an anchor here so you can't run back to the ranch?" Kitty asked.

"Absolutely," Bella said.

"Fantastic. Motivation is everything." Kitty grinned. "The beauty of being a wealthy woman is that you can make choices like that. Own the fact you have options, Bella. Let's go find Diana. We'll be delighted to work with you, right Piper?"

"Of course we are." Piper was frowning though. "Are you sure you want to do this? I mean, don't buy a business just because you want to anchor yourself here. At least buy one you want to do."

Bella was restless. "I know how to cook. It will be great. Let's go." She wanted an anchor. She wanted something for herself. A business that wasn't tied to her family. *Something* for herself.

Piper sighed. "Bella, it's amazing to have a business you really care about. Hold out for it."

"I don't have any other skills," Bella blurted out. "I don't know how to do anything but cook, ride horses, and be a sister. This is what I can do. I'm doing it." She felt like crying right now, she was so desperate. She wanted to feel excitement, but all she felt was absolute desperation. "Where's Diana, Kitty? Can you introduce us? I want to get it done tonight."

Piper shook her head. "You can't just sign a contract. You need a lawyer to look at it—"

"I know." This was one area Bella knew what she was doing. The Harts had come from so little, that they'd all been very vigilant about educating themselves about money and contracts. "The Harts don't sign any contract without having it vetted. We'll get the letter of intent tonight, then hammer out the details." She looked at Kitty. "Ready?"

"Yep." Kitty shot Piper a look and then took Bella's arm. "She's in the kitchen. Let's go, honey. Owning a business feels amazing. You'll love it."

Bella nodded, nerves gripping her belly as she let Kitty

lead her toward the kitchen. She knew she wasn't ready to own a business, to decide she wanted to be in food, but she also knew if she waited until she was ready, she'd never change anything about her life.

Falcon raised his brows, and she pointed toward the swinging doors. "We're going to the kitchen to make a deal."

He fell in beside them, accompanying them. "You're buying it?"

"Yes."

"You sure about that?"

"No."

To her surprise, her answer made him smile. "Good. Take a risk you can afford. It always pays off, even when it fails."

That reaction, that belief, made something inside her settle. On some level at least, maybe recklessly buying a small business she didn't even want made sense, even if she didn't know how at this time.

As she thought it, she realized he was right.

She was going to own her own business. Not her family's. Hers.

It felt good. Empowering. Liberating. Scary, but also... freaking awesome.

Then she looked over at Falcon, and saw a grim expression flit across his face. He saw her looking and replaced the grimness with a smile that almost went to his eyes.

Almost.

TWENTY-TWO

SEVERAL HOURS LATER, at the end of the evening, Falcon leaned against the doorframe to the little office that Bella and Diana were meeting in. Bella had her lawyer on speakerphone, and she was handling the negotiations like a woman who knew what she was doing.

She was strong, confident, and impressive as hell.

He didn't understand why she felt she was living small. She was a powerful force in every moment.

Vulnerable with him as well, but that vulnerability didn't make her weak. Maybe it added to her power.

Why couldn't she see herself the way he saw her? The way she was?

"All right, then," Bella said, hanging up the phone. "We have ourselves a deal. My lawyer will email the letter of intent shortly, and I'll send it on to you after I read it. We'll sign in the morning."

Diana clapped her hands. "This is fantastic. I created this business with my daughter. She got married and moved to Chicago to open a gourmet ice cream truck there. It's going so well that she wants to add three more trucks. She's been asking me to move out there and help with the business, but I couldn't leave unless I got the right offer, which is you. I'm using this money to invest in her business and move out there to help her with it." She hugged Bella. "Thank you for making our dreams come true!" She grabbed her phone. "I'm going to call her now. She'll be so excited!"

Diana hugged Falcon, and then headed off down the hall. "Sweetie? It's Mom! We have the money!"

Falcon grinned as Diana shrieked into the phone. "Damn, they're happy. That's so cool you made her dreams come true."

Bella was smiling, too. "She's so happy. That's so amazing." She looked at Falcon. "It's amazing what a difference money can make. I could have just given her daughter the money and invested in the business if I'd known."

"It's more fun to earn it. They'll have a great time. Did you see their bond? It's about family for them."

Bella's smile faded as she watched Diana disappear around the corner. "It is, isn't it?" She looked at Falcon. "Am I making a mistake? Walking away from family? I don't want to walk away from them. I love them. They're my whole world. I just—" She stopped. "What am I doing, Falcon? I spent so much of my life alone and now I have a family, and I want to walk away from them?"

"No." He put his arm over her shoulder, pulling her in close. "You're not walking away from them. You're adding to your life."

"By trapping myself here? A catering business is an on-site business. I have to be here to run it. What if I don't want to be here? What if I want to go home?" Her voice rose in panic.

"Hey." He put his hands on her shoulders. "Take a breath, sweetheart."

"I can't! I just agreed to buy a business I don't even know if I want! I'm used to freedom. And now I can't leave!"

Falcon couldn't help it. He started laughing.

"What?" She shoved at his chest. "You're *laughing* at me?"

He caught her wrists. "No, Bella. I'm laughing with you. You're trying to be brave, and it's scary. That's normal. It's all good."

"It's not good."

"It is." He pressed a kiss to her knuckles. "I'll be honest. It's scary as hell letting myself get involved with you, but I'm not going anywhere."

Bella stared at him, then she started laughing. "I'm like a catering business?"

He grinned when she laughed, knowing he'd broken through her panic. "You're exactly like a catering business. That's what I was thinking this afternoon when my soul was falling into your eyes."

Her smile widened. "Is that what was happening?"

"It was. I was thinking, am I drowning in her eyes, or are the croissants ready for serving? It's confusing for a guy like me who has been outside the world of plated food for so long."

She giggled. "Plates and utensils can be so confusing."

"Right? You get me." He pulled her in for a kiss. "I love how you get me, Bella. It's so refreshing not to have to pretend I know how to sit at a table."

She put her arms around his neck. "Falcon, no one would look at you and expect *you* to know how to sit at a table."

"No? What would they expect?" He backed her into the wall, leaning his hips against hers.

"A wild animal scavenging for food in the dark of night?"

"Hmm...I like that." He bent his head and nibbled on her neck. "We're the last ones here, Bella. Maybe we should celebrate your business deal."

She leaned her head back to give him access. "Champagne and strawberries?"

"I thought I saw some whipped cream in the fridge."

She wrinkled her nose. "That's just sticky."

He slid his hand behind her neck. "No whipped cream then."

She caught her breath as he began to nibble on her lower lip. "I didn't bring the condoms."

He grinned. "I did."

She started laughing. "Seriously?"

"Yeah. If someone comes after you, we might have to go on the run. I didn't want to be stranded in a safehouse with you without proper protection."

"Protection? Like your gun?"

"Exactly like my gun." Then he leaned in and showed her exactly what kind of protection she needed. And she quickly made it clear that it was the kind of protection she liked.

A perfect pair.

For now.

Until the inherent conflicts between them made it impossible to have a future together, of course.

But he'd worry about that later.

Much, much later.

Because right now, he had to protect her.

Because that's what good bodyguards did.

TWENTY-THREE

THE NEXT MORNING, Bella woke up restless and unsettled.

It was still dark, but Falcon wasn't in the bed either.

She frowned as she sat up, trying to figure out why she was upset. Not merely because Falcon wasn't there, right? She wasn't already dependent on him, was she?

No. Of course not. They'd had some highly personal intimacy at the event hall, and then had gone out for drinks afterwards. He'd made her laugh, and she'd made him laugh. They'd traded stories about the bridge days, and she'd regaled him with tales about crazy dude ranch guests.

They'd danced in the shadowy corner to a jukebox, romantic and slow.

It had been a perfect date night...its perfection preserved by the fact they had stayed away from any inflammatory topics. She hadn't asked him to talk about the revenge quest he'd been on for so long. Neither of them had discussed kids or marriage or the Hart Ranch, or her soon-to-be-acquired business.

It had been light and fun. The way dating should be at the start with someone.

Except they weren't at the start, even though they were.

What were they doing?

Her phone dinged, and she rolled over to look at it. It was the email from her attorney, with the letter of intent and the first draft of the contract.

Her stomach sank. Diana's catering business. Which she'd promised a lot of money for. Which she was going to own shortly.

"Argh!" She flopped back down in bed and pulled the pillow over her face. Did she want it? No. Did she? Maybe? Was she just scared? Shouldn't she be excited? Or maybe she was excited, but her mind was trying to convince her she wasn't.

She should have just given Diana the money. Invested in the trucks. Then she could co-own a business without having to actually do anything with it.

But that was just money.

It didn't change *her*.

It didn't give *her* a purpose.

It funded someone else's purpose, but didn't give *her* one.

Unless her purpose was to fund other people's dreams?

That felt empty. Too distant to make an impact. Too... Argh!

Her phone rang, but it was Brody's ringtone, so she had to answer. She rolled onto her side and picked up. "It's awfully early out there."

"Is Falcon with you?"

She sat up quickly, alarmed by Brody's urgent tone. "I assume he's in the living room."

"Go get him. I need to talk to the two of you together."

Her heart started racing, and she threw the covers back. "What? What's going on?"

"We tracked the guys who were at your house. They're related to Falcon's quest. You're both in danger. They know where your cottage is. You guys need to get out fast."

Crap. She ran into the living room. "Falcon!"

He wasn't there.

Frowning, she checked the kitchen and the bathroom. "He's—" She paused, not wanting to give Brody a reason to go all patriarchal on her. "He's in the bathroom. Tell me what's going on and I'll relay it."

"Call me when you're on the road. Just get out fast."

"Right. Will do." Bella hung up and shoved the phone in her pocket. There was no way Falcon would be out of the house right now, not when he was in bodyguard mode.

But he wasn't inside.

Fear tried to creep down her spine, but years of practice enabled her to shut it down and focus. She ran into the bedroom and got her gun, a penlight, her wallet, and her keys.

Survival mode had been ingrained in her since she was a little kid, and old habits flared back to life like she'd never had a break.

The familiar state of mind felt safe...and awful at the same time. She hated that she was so capable of stepping up when she was in danger. Well, not that. She hated that she was so used to being in danger that it wasn't a second thought.

Her car was by the front door, but she headed to the bathroom, raised the window, and slipped outside, landing silently in the darkness.

If someone was waiting for her to come out the front door, they were going to have to wait.

She crouched in the shadows under the window, listening for the sound of an intruder, but all she could hear was the gentle crashing of the waves on the beach...beautiful, and also so useful for drowning out footsteps for the bad guys.

She pulled out her phone and texted Falcon. "Where are you?"

No reply.

Crap.

She inched around the side of the house, and she saw her car only a few yards away. It was in the light from the side of the cottage, and she could see there was no one around it. She could zip right over there and drive away to safety.

But where was Falcon?

He hadn't left her. She was sure of it.

Which meant something had happened to him.

Sudden tension gripped her chest, and she had to fight harder to keep her focus. "No. He's safe," she whispered. "He'd want you to leave."

But she couldn't make herself just drive away. What if he was in trouble?

Then he'd want her to leave.

Except that no one got to tell her what to do anymore. Even Falcon.

Dammit.

She eased back against the side of the house and made her way around the other side, toward the beach, scanning the dusky moonlight rays for any sign of Falcon.

But nothing.

Just a silent, empty oceanside cottage.

Fear began to rise in her. She'd lost before. She couldn't lose again. *She couldn't.*

She eased around the corner of the house toward the beach, then immediately ducked back into the shadows. Two dark shapes were stretched out on the beach, not moving. Men? Falcon?

Oh, God.

She paused to scan the beach, looking for any signs of anyone else, but she sensed nothing. No one.

She was an idiot to do this. She knew she was. Except Falcon was hers, and she never left anyone behind. None of the Harts did.

Gun ready, she took a breath, and then burst out of the shadows and sprinted across the sand.

Two men were face down in the sand.

One was a man she didn't know, all in black. His face was battered—from Falcon's fists? He was utterly motionless. Dead? She had a bad feeling.

The other was Falcon. His eyes were closed, his face was also battered, and he had blood spreading on his T-shirt on his left side.

Oh, *God*. She crouched beside him, scanning the beach. "Falcon," she whispered. "Wake up."

He didn't move.

She put her hand in front of his mouth, and felt the movement of his breath.

Alive.

She needed to get them out of there. Men like the one Falcon had fought with rarely worked alone. And someone would at least know he was there. "Falcon!" She shoved his shoulder, and he groaned.

Yes. "Get up," she whispered. "We're in danger. Get up."

His eyes snapped open, and he lunged to his feet, then stumbled and almost fell. "They found us. We gotta go."

"I know." She threw his arm over her shoulder so she could support him, but he didn't lean on her. He shoved her to his left side so his gun hand was free, still in protector mode.

Both of them with their guns ready, they made it across the sand as fast as his compromised body would allow, continuously scanning the beach.

"My car. I'll drive," she said.

"Mine. It's got supplies."

Of course it had supplies. The man had lived on the run for twenty years, and she'd gotten soft. "Okay. I'm driving."

He didn't argue with that one, and he almost fell into the passenger seat when she got him in it. She helped him belt in, then ran around to the driver's side, jumped in, and started the truck.

She hit the gas, peeling out as she whipped the truck around, over the lawn, and raced out onto the main road. Falcon gripped the door to keep from sliding, continuously looking out the back window while she drove.

After about ten minutes of tense silence, he turned forward again. "Only one guy today."

"Did you kill him?"

"No. I don't think so. Maybe." He closed his eyes. "The fucker stabbed me. I heard him working on the front door and when I went to get him, he stabbed me."

"Did you stab him back?"

"Didn't have a knife. But I can kill a man with my pinkie, so it was fine." He closed his eyes. "You good?"

"Fantastic." How had she not heard that fight? How had she slept through it? Years of sleeping on the ranch had made her too relaxed, apparently. This was why she wanted to be off the ranch? So she could have someone try to stab her?

Oh, wait, they'd broken into the ranch first. So, safety outside. No, they'd found her here, too. So, safety nowhere. "Do you need a doctor?"

"Don't know. I need to check it." He swore and pressed his hand to his side. "I have first aid in the back seat. I just need a sec."

She glanced over at him, her heart tightening. "Don't you dare die on me."

"No. Never. I'll die beside you. I weigh too much to die on you. You'd be trapped and that's no good."

She couldn't help the giggle that squeaked out. "You're crazy."

"Yep. A crazy monster. I didn't recognize the guy."

Oh, right. "Brody called. He said the guys who were in my house were connected to your quest."

Falcon went silent, and the energy in the truck suddenly became so dense she couldn't breathe. "Falcon?"

"I'm calling Brody. I need to know what he found out."

129

"Falcon, this isn't your fault."

"It sure as fuck is. Imagine if I had kids? I'd put them all in danger. Every single person who I love." Grief was thick in his voice. "Good thing I didn't make the mistake of starting a family, right? I'd have to abandon them, and we all know how much that sucks as a kid to be abandoned."

Tears filled Bella's eyes. "Falcon—"

"I'm fine. Moving on. I accept my path."

"No. Don't! We don't need to accept anything!"

He ignored her, pulled out his phone, and hit send. "I'm calling Brody—"

She whacked the phone out of his hand. "No, you're not."

He looked over at her, his gaze hooded, his face pinched with pain. "Bella—"

"Shut up. I'm in charge now." She looked over at him. "I'm finding a place to park, and then we're going to deal with this. Right now."

"With what?"

She gestured randomly in his direction. "This. All of *this*. Now."

TWENTY-FOUR

FALCON WAS in too much pain to argue with Bella.

He trusted her to make a good choice to lay low, so he used the time to twist around in his seat and get his medical bag. The movement was brutal, but he forced the pain aside.

It had been a while since he'd been stabbed, and he'd forgotten how much it hurt.

By the time he got himself cleaned, inspected, and bandaged, he was sweating from the pain. "I'm getting too old for this," he muttered under his breath as he tossed the medical bag on the floor between his feet.

He closed his eyes and leaned back, then opened them when the truck bumped over something. He started laughing when he realized they were pulling into the local police station. "The local cops are no match for these guys."

"I know, but they'll have cameras in the parking lot, and our friends won't like the cameras." She pulled up right in front of the door, switched off the engine and turned to face him. "Do you need a doctor?"

He grinned. This woman thought she was small? She was a beast, and he loved it. "No. I don't think he got anything important, and I cleaned it."

"Antibiotics?"

"I already took one."

She raised her brows. "You dispense your own prescription drugs?"

"I do. It hasn't been safe for me to go to the doctor for a long time." Falcon swore under his breath, and punched his fist lightly against the dashboard as the reality of the situation sank in. "It's me, then. I endangered you. I'd endanger any kids."

The realization hit like a spike in his chest. No kids. No wife. No family. He would never risk anyone just because he wanted the life he'd never had. "I'll walk away when this is over. I'll stay away from you. From the ranch. I'll disappear and no one will be able to link us again—"

She put her finger on his lips. "Shut up."

He moved her hand, wrapping his fingers around hers. "Bella," he said gently. "This possibility was why I stayed away for so long. I thought it was over." He kissed her knuckles. "I'm sorry, Bella. With all of my heart. I'm so fucking sorry for endangering you by coming for you."

She ignored his apology. "Tell me about this quest that you've been tangled up in for so long."

He shook his head. "It doesn't matter—"

"Falcon. You made love to me a whole bunch of times. You told me you loved me. You don't get to pretend that didn't happen, and since it's me, you don't get to be a jerk and walk away. You lost the right to lock me out. So talk to me." Her voice was gentle, but urgent, and the look on her face made his heart turn over.

She wanted to know. She wanted him to let her in.

He still had to leave. He knew he did.

But sitting there in that truck with her, blood soaking through his shirt, knowing how close he'd come to losing her if he'd been sleeping when that guy had showed up, knowing that he could never have the family with her that he'd dreamed of for so long…suddenly, he needed this moment as much as she did.

He needed to be seen by the woman he loved before he disappeared forever.

He took a breath and steeled himself. "When I was growing up, it was just my mom and me. When she wasn't using, she was a good mom. She gave me everything she had."

Bella's mouth opened, and then she closed it and nodded. "What was her name?"

"Jenny." He didn't give the last name. He never did.

"Jenny," Bella repeated. "I'm glad you had her for a while."

Of course it had been only a while. If he'd still had her, he never would have wound up on the streets under a bridge with the Harts. "She got clean when I was six. Got me back from foster and worked hard to stay clean. Drug addiction is brutal, Bella. Every day was a fight for her, but she was stronger than it." He paused. "For me. She told me every day that I was her light, her reason for staying clean. I tried to be the best kid I could to make her want to stay clean even more. I lived for making her happy."

Bella's face softened. "That's a heavy burden for a kid."

He shrugged. "It didn't feel heavy. It gave me a purpose. We lived in a shitty area and it kept me clean and out of trouble, unlike most kids."

She smiled. "Always a huge heart, even back then."

"Desperate to never go back to foster care, yeah." He paused, taking a breath before he continued. "When I was ten, a man showed up at our door. From her past." He closed his eyes, trying to shield himself from the anger that still rose, from the terror he'd felt back then.

Then he felt Bella take his hand, her grip grounding him. He looked down at their entangled hands, and closed his hand around hers. "He was an absolute shit. All the worst things you can imagine? He did it."

Bella rubbed his hand. "Tell me."

He took a breath. "One day I came home from school, and my mom was strung out. He'd gotten her back on drugs." He'd been so mad that day. So fucking furious. "She'd been clean for four years. Do you know how hard that was? And he fucking tore it all down."

Bella nodded. "My mom was a drug addict too. Her boyfriend was why I ran away."

His gaze shot to hers, and suddenly, he was tired of feeling like shit because of a bastard when he was a little kid. They'd all been through things. Why was he hanging onto it like he was the only one? "I went after him. He knocked me around, and then my mom attacked him to save me. He killed her in front of me, and left me to die."

Bella's hand went to her mouth. "Oh, God. Falcon."

"I held my mom in my arms and I promised her I would live, and I would avenge her death. I told her I'd stay clean, I'd never get addicted to anything, I'd be the man she wanted me to become, and I would make sure that he never hurt anyone ever again."

Understanding filled Bella's face, a compassionate, true understanding that answered a need that he hadn't realized he'd had until now. "That's who you've been hunting for twenty years?" she asked, without any judgment.

He nodded. "It was a game to him. He thought it was funny. When I was a teenager, he would catch me and beat me up. Then I learned to hide when I was hunting him. And he got better at hiding. Until someone else got to him and ended it."

"Who was he?"

He looked at Bella. "He was my biological father, Bella. His blood runs in my veins. His monster is in my DNA. I—"

"No." She grabbed his shoulders. "There is no monster in

you, Falcon. There *isn't*. You are light and sunshine, and that's why your mom was able to stay clean. For you. Because you're a healer, remember?"

"I couldn't heal her. Not from drugs, not from putting up with an asshole, and not from the knife he used on her." He looked down at his hands that always burned so much. "For a healer, I couldn't do it when it mattered. So, even if I am one, so what? If I couldn't do it for her, I'll never be able to do it for anyone."

Bella put her hands over his. "You were a little boy," she said softly. "In survival mode. And you became a man who never forgot the promise he made to his mom to avenge her, and to be the amazing human being you promised her you'd be."

He squeezed her hands. "When I found him dead, I thought it was over. I don't know who picked up the game, but I'm tired of it," he admitted. "I don't want to do it anymore, but I have to." He raised her hands and kissed them. "I have to keep going for you, Bella. I had to start it for her, and I will keep going for you."

She shook her head. "I don't want you to keep going."

"Me either, but I can't let someone hurt you." He shrugged. "It's my path. My destiny. I accept it."

"No. You don't have to accept anything. Our destinies are never predetermined. No matter how long you have lived a certain life, you can always change it."

He gestured at his bloody shirt. "Some lives won't let you go."

She pulled back and put her hands on her hips. "Are you serious? You're going to roll over for some life you don't want? Why would you do that? You want to get married and a have a family—"

"I will *not* endanger anyone—"

"Hire Dylan. He has a team of badasses who will hunt whoever this is down and get rid of him—"

"It's *my* problem."

"No, it's not! It was never your problem! You made it your problem, and now you have enough money to make it someone else's problem." She hit her palm on the steering wheel. "Why are you being so stubborn, Falcon? Just pay someone who's trained for it, has the resources, and who *wants* to do it. How long do you think you'll last going out there this time, when you don't want to? You got stabbed already. What if there were two? Or three? Or you were asleep? Do you *want* to die?"

"No!" He was shocked by her question. "I'd never betray all those who don't get to live, by choosing death."

"Well, you're choosing to give up your dreams, and your mom sacrificed herself so you could live. And now you're going to keep living in darkness? Would she want that?"

He stared at her, stunned by her words. "Don't use my mom against me."

"I'm not! I'm using her *for* you. She's not here to tell you not to make her sacrifice mean nothing. She would want you to live, and love, and thrive, wouldn't she? Not to spend your whole life in revenge and then whatever this is you're planning to do now."

Anger coiled through him. "You don't know anything about my mom."

"I know what you told me about her, and I know that despite all her demons, she managed to raise a man who has a heart of gold, is a freaking *healer* meant to bring light into the world—"

Dammit. He wished he'd never told her about the healer. "I'm not a fucking healer, Bella. I told you."

She threw up her hands in visible frustration. "No, you're not. Not if you decide you're not."

"I tried—"

"Did you?" She turned toward him. "I'd give anything to find my path. My identity. My purpose. You've been given yours: healer. And you're just making up excuses not to step into it. What are you so scared of, Falcon?"

"I'm scared of you dying."

She blinked. "What?"

"My mom died. She was all I had. She died because of me, because I attacked him and she had to save me. You've been my heart since I met you. If you die because of me, then...I've done it twice."

"Oh, *Falcon.*" Bella's eyes widened, and her eyes glistened with tears. "You've been blaming yourself all this time?"

He shrugged. "I take responsibility. It's not complicated." Fuck, his side hurt. He closed his eyes, trying to keep the truck from spinning.

He felt her hand on his face. "Falcon. Are you okay?"

"Nope." He took a breath, and it hurt. "I think you should call Brody. I don't think I can protect you right now, and since I basically live to keep you safe, I'm not loving that fact."

"Brody? He'll make us go back to the ranch."

"I knew I'd get you back there one way or another." He laughed softly, and then swore as pain shot through him. "Can't go to a hospital, Bella. Can't protect you. Brody will know what to do. Call him. It's time."

The words had barely left Falcon's lips when his head lolled to the side, and he slumped over.

"Falcon!" Bella shook his shoulder, but there was no reaction. "Shit. Shit. Shit." She grabbed her phone and dialed her brother, who answered immediately.

"Are you guys safe?"

"Falcon got stabbed. Some guy is on the beach in front of the cottage, maybe dead. We're in Falcon's truck in front of the police station, and he just passed out. He said he's fine, and he treated it, but he's now unconscious so—" She had to stop to keep the panic out of her voice.

"Head to the airport," Brody said immediately. "I'll have the plane ready, and I'll have a doctor there."

"The plane?"

"Yeah, I sent it yesterday as soon as your house was invaded. It's been there waiting in case you needed a fast exit."

Tears filled her eyes as she started the truck. "Most of the time, I'd be super annoyed with you for doing that, but right now, I'm happy. I'm freaking out, Brody," she admitted. "What if Falcon dies?"

"He won't die. He hasn't married you yet."

She started laughing through her tears as she pulled up driving directions to the airport. "He won't marry me. He's going to get me safe and then abandon me forever so I don't get killed by his enemies."

"Heroic man. I admire him. How do you feel about that?"

"Before he got stabbed, he wanted to get married, have kids, and live on the ranch." She pulled out onto the main road and hit the gas, keeping vigilant for any headlight suddenly appearing behind her.

"No good?"

"I don't want that, Brody." But she looked over at Falcon. *I don't want to lose you, Falcon.* But wanting him to live wasn't the same thing as being ready to give up her dreams and move back to the ranch to become a wife and mother. But right now, it felt so twisted up she couldn't really think straight.

"I figured as much," Brody said. "I told him I wasn't sure you guys would be compatible. So it's working out fine."

"Fine? He's unconscious and bleeding."

"He's not dead, so it all works. I need to make some calls. I'm tracking you, and if anything alerts you, call back. I'm trying to find you an escort to the airport, but not sure I can find someone I trust so quick. Stay vigilant."

"Okay, I will." She pulled her gun free and held it in her right hand. Ready. "I love you, Brody. I'm sorry I left."

"I love you too, Bella, and never be sorry for being who you are. Our family can never be broken. You know that. Talk soon." Then he hung up.

Bella gripped the steering wheel and hit the gas. "Falcon," she said, over the roar of the engine. "I know you're unconscious and can't hear me, but I want to tell you that I love you. I have always loved you, and that's probably why nothing has ever worked out with anyone else." She took a breath. "I believe you're a healer, Falcon. And by healing others, you'll heal yourself. And the world needs you healed." She paused. "*I* need you healed, Falcon."

She fell quiet as the truck kept speeding down the empty road.

"And Falcon, I am so very sorry that I can't marry you." As she spoke, a heavy weight settled in her chest. "You'll make the best dad, but I could never be the wife and mother you want. I can't live up to your dreams, and I'm sorry about that."

So incredibly sorry, in ways she couldn't even process.

The man had dreams, and she wasn't the woman who could fulfill them.

And she wouldn't let him give up on his dreams, just like she knew he'd never let her give up on hers.

But first, he had to survive.

After that? She had an idea...which he was definitely going to hate.

TWENTY-FIVE

FALCON ROLLED OVER IN BED, then frowned when he saw the Hart Ranch out the window.

What the hell?

He sat up, then grimaced as pain shot through his side. Right. The stabbing. Vague memories passed through his mind of being on the plane, and having some woman treating him. Hart family doctor, maybe?

And now he was here. Was Bella also? Had she come back to the ranch with him?

Bella.

Was she safe?

He shoved the covers back and lurched to his feet, pressing his hand to his side. He wasn't in the guest room in Brody's house or any of the others he'd been in. Which Hart house was he in?

He forced himself to stand up straight and strode across the room, jerked the door open, and stepped out into the hall. "Bella!"

"You're up! In here, Falcon!"

Relief rushed through him at the sound of her cheerful voice. She was alive, and sounded fine. He walked down the hall, hand still pressed to his side. When he walked out into the main living area, he immediately recognized the big white couches, the adjoining professional-grade kitchen, and the big picture windows that looked out on the ranch.

He was in Bella's house.

Yes.

"How do you feel?"

He turned toward the sound of her voice as she walked around the corner from the back of the house. He was pretty sure she had an office back there. She was wearing black leggings, a baggy pink sweatshirt, and pink fuzzy socks.

She looked absolutely adorable, and he couldn't stop his smile. "I feel great. You?"

She raised her brows. "You look pasty and wan. Sit down and let me feed you." She pointed to a chair at the kitchen island.

"No hug?"

She paused. "You want a hug?"

"For a start." He moved gingerly across the room, smiling as she frowned at him.

"I think you're a little too injured."

"No such thing." He caught her wrist, pulled her toward him, and kissed her. Not a kiss to seduce. A kiss to connect. To wind their souls together. He knew he had to leave, but seeing her made him want to do nothing but fall into her kiss and never leave.

Bella immediately wrapped her arms around his neck and kissed him back without hesitation.

Her response settled his edginess, and when the kiss ended, he continued to hold her, resting his forehead against hers as pain throbbed through his side. "I was afraid you'd be pissed at me."

She closed her eyes. "For getting stabbed? I am. I thought you might die, and I wasn't happy about it."

"I promise not to die."

STEPHANIE ROWE

She searched his gaze. "Don't make promises you can't keep."

"I always keep my promises." He kissed the tip of her nose. "I thought you'd be mad that my injury forced you to come back to the ranch."

"Forced me?" She shook her head. "No one ever makes me do anything." She wrapped her fingers in the front of his T-shirt. "I chose to come. You would have been fine if I'd put you on the plane alone."

He considered that. "And you would have gone back to the cottage?"

"Well, no." She shrugged and released his shirt. "But I'm good at disappearing. I would have been fine alone. I made a choice, Falcon. I always choose."

He caught her wrist as she began to turn away, drawing her back to him. "Well, then, thank you," he said softly. "Thank you for taking charge, getting us out of there, and for coming back to the ranch for me." He pressed a kiss to her hand. "I know it wasn't what you wanted, and you did it anyway. Thank you."

Her face softened. "You're very welcome, Falcon. I'd never let you down. You know that."

"I do." He took a breath. "I never let myself be a burden to anyone. I never put myself in a position where anyone needs to help me, but last night, I fucked up, and I had to count on you." He paused. "I can't even express what it feels like to have someone take care of me like that. I—" He didn't have words. "I'll never forget it," he finally said.

Bella smiled tenderly. "You are a very sweet man." She patted his cheek. "Let me feed you, please. I hate seeing you so pale." She pulled out a chair. "Sit those cute little butt cheeks on there, please."

Falcon grinned and eased himself down on the seat. "I assume there have been security upgrades to your house?"

142

"Of course. No one could get in now. We're safe." She walked over to the stove and began making him an omelet.

She'd put in all his favorite ingredients, he noticed. She'd remembered what he liked and had made the effort to get everything for him in the few hours they'd been home.

He smiled. Bella might not want to be a wife or a mom, but her nurturing side was beautiful to him.

"What are you grinning at?" she asked, tossing him a sassy look.

"Your ass looks great in those leggings. Want to get naked later?"

She rolled her eyes. "You're moving so stiffly that I don't think you'd be able to handle me."

"Try me."

"No." She was quiet for a minute. "I did some things you might not like."

He leaned back in the seat, feeling immensely relaxed with her. He knew they were fully protected on the ranch, and he didn't have to be on guard. This was what had kept him going for all those years. The vision of breakfast on the ranch with Bella. Just the two of them.

And now he was living it.

He knew it was fleeting, but he was going to burn every detail into his mind so he would never forget it.

She looked over. "Did you hear me?"

Oh, right. He focused on the conversation. "I did. It's fine. When I blew my bodyguard duty, I forfeited the right to be annoyed with anything you do." When he fell in love with her, he also forfeited that in some ways, but he wasn't going to mention that.

She flipped the omelet. "Well, first, let's get things straight. You didn't fail at being a bodyguard. You took down a man coming to get us. Yes, you got stabbed in the process, but you saved the day, so take a little bit of pride in that, please."

He grinned. "All right. I'll admit that. Did you find out who he was?" He had no doubt that Brody made some calls, and that man had been tracked down before he'd gotten very far.

"Well, that's one of the things I want to talk to you about." She put the omelet in front of him, along with a coffee and utensils.

"Thank you for the breakfast." He leaned over, caught her chin, and kissed her. "I appreciate it. You know that your omelets are the best in the entire world, and I'm honored you made it for me."

She smiled and kissed him back. "You're very welcome. And thank you for the compliment. I accept it."

He kissed her for another moment, until his growling stomach made them both laugh. She pointed at the plate, and he sank back down onto the chair.

"Yes, ma'am." He took a bite, and had to close his eyes. "Hell, this is incredible."

"We have so many fresh vegetables and herbs in the garden right now," she said. "It makes such a difference." She paused, and he felt her tension rise. "I hired Dylan to track down the men who broke into my house and the guy who stabbed you."

He paused, his fork halfway to his mouth. "What?"

"I don't want you running around the world getting stabbed," she said, searching his face. "You fulfilled your promise to your mom, Falcon. It's over. I paid Dylan to take over. He already has his best team on it. They'll find out what's going on soon. In the meantime, you can just stay here and recover."

He put his fork down, tension wrapping around him. "No."

She lifted her chin. "Yes."

Tension coiled through him. "This is my legacy, Bella. You don't get to take it from me."

She frowned. "It's not your legacy! Starting another

144

revenge quest is an excuse not to live. The man who killed your mom is dead. He's *dead*. It's *over*."

"It's not over! Someone came after you. Twice!" He pushed back. "I can't sit around eating. I have to get started. I have to go—" He stopped when tears glistened in Bella's eyes. "Bella—"

She shook her head and held up her hand to silence him. "You don't get to choose to die anymore, Falcon. You made me fall in love with you again, and when you did that, you forfeited the right to go do stupid, unnecessary things that are going to get you killed."

He stared at her, stunned. "You fell in love with me again?"

"I did. And guess what? You aren't the only one who suffered loss as a kid. I did, too. I don't trust anyone but my family. And you made me trust you again, so your choices are no longer only about you." She put her hand on her heart. "I thought you were dying," she whispered. "I thought you were dying right next to me in that truck. It was awful, Falcon."

Shit. He ran his hand through his hair. "I'm sorry—"

She didn't give him a chance to speak, talking right over him. "You know the Harts protect each other, Falcon. You've been gone for a long time, but the rules still apply. You don't get to risk your life anymore. Brody and Dylan agreed with me. It's over. It's done. We're taking it away from you."

The tears streaming down her cheeks made it impossible for him to be angry at her. But… "If someone on Dylan's team dies because they took over my issue—"

"Stop!" She held up her hands. "Just stop, Falcon. They're professionals!"

"I know but—"

She interrupted him. "It's just one excuse after another, isn't it? You don't really want to get married and have kids, do you? It's your dream, but you'll always have an excuse not to do it, won't you? Because at the end of the day, you're more scared than I am."

He stared at her. "I'm not scared. I'm a protector. I need to protect you."

"No." She tossed her spatula on the counter. "*Brody* is a protector. He steps into life fully. You're just using the danger as an excuse to run from life, and from those who love you, who would have given you the home you lost so long ago."

Tension coiled inside him. "I'm not running from life."

"No? What if I told you I'd marry you? Right now? This second. What would you say?"

His breath caught in his chest. "You want to marry me?"

She froze and then lifted her chin. "Falcon, will you marry me? Right now? Brody will marry us. He has a license."

The tension in the air was so thick he could taste it.

This moment, this woman, it was everything he'd ever dreamed of.

She waited, watching him. "Falcon?"

He swore under his breath. "I can't. Not until it's safe."

"Of course not." Hurt flashed across her face. "You never would have married me, would you? You always would have found a reason."

"That's not true—"

"Are you so sure about that?"

At her challenge, he paused. Was she right? He trusted Bella's judgment. What did she see that he didn't?

When he didn't answer, she tossed a sponge at him. "This is why I don't date. This is why I'll never get married. Because even the men I should be able to trust, aren't worth it. When you were unconscious, I told you that I loved you, but that I couldn't marry you because I could never be the wife and mother you dreamed of. But I take that back. I'll never marry you, because you can't be the man I deserve. Clean up after you finish eating. I'm going for a ride. Don't follow me. Just...don't."

Then she turned and walked out the back door, leaving him at the kitchen counter.

He wanted to go after her.

He wanted to haul ass after her, drop to his knees, and ask her to marry him properly. To show he was the man she deserved.

But he didn't move.

Because life had taught him that she was dead right.

TWENTY-SIX

BELLA RODE HARD, not stopping until she reached her destination, a hidden oasis her family had named Hart's Pond. She patted her horse's neck as she slowed to a stop beside the beautiful spot. "Thanks, Honey." She hopped off, removed Honey's saddle, cooled the mare down, and then turned her loose in the pen they'd built out there for that exact purpose.

She checked Honey's water, gave her some hay, and then walked to the edge of the pond.

She sat down on the flat rock she'd used so many times for a picnic for herself and hugged her knees to her chest.

The late morning sun was bright, but Honey's pen was in the shade, keeping her cool.

The sun reflected off the crystal-clear water, and she could see all the way to the bottom of the pond.

Bella rested her chin on her knees, rocking gently, waiting for the energy of Hart's Pond to work its magic. After a few moments, she felt herself begin to relax, and she was able to finally take a deep breath.

"Men," she muttered.

"What about them?"

She jumped and turned to see Tatum Crosby, Brody's wife, and her sister Meg emerging from the opening in the thick foliage that surrounded the pool. She sighed when she saw them, not in the mood for company. "Uh, hi. I was just on my way home." She headed over toward Honey to make her lie the truth.

"I stopped by to see you," Meg said. "Falcon was sitting in your kitchen looking very stabbed and contemplative. He said you took off and said not to follow, so I figured you came here."

Bella frowned. "How did you get here so fast?"

"I drove," Phoebe Hart, the wife of her brother Jacob, walked in, accompanied by Sofia, who was married to Keegan. "We were heading into town for brunch, and we stopped to grab you and Meg. She said you were on a walkabout, so we figured you needed some girl time."

Bella sighed. "I'm just leaving—"

"Nope, you're not." Meg put her arm around her. "We have champagne and snacks. It's party time."

"I'm not in the mood—"

"Really?" Tatum put her hands on her hips. "Brody told me that you wanted to move to Boston because of Maddie's friends. Because you wanted more than your brothers."

Bella felt her gut drop. "I didn't mean it like that. I love you guys—"

"I know." Tatum adjusted her cowboy hat. "Here's the thing. I'm away a lot at my residency in Vegas and other concerts. I was excited to connect with you and Meg again, but I'm not around a lot."

Bella shrugged. Tatum had been an under-the-bridge kid at one point, and then she'd taken off without a good-bye. None of the Harts had heard from her since then, until one day Tatum had sent Brody a ticket and asked him to come to her concert.

Bella had loved Tatum as a big sister, and Tatum had left

her. The pain was still there, commingled with all her other trust issues. But that was fine. Tatum made Brody happy and that was all that mattered. Besides, Tatum was a freaking international superstar. She was amazing. "You have an incredible career. I think that's awesome," she said honestly.

"Tablecloth is set," Phoebe called out. "Come on, ladies. Let's drink and eat."

Bella glanced over at the rock, and then blinked in surprise when she saw the beautiful display that Phoebe and Sofia had already set up. There was a thick blanket, a flower centerpiece, and even nice plates and silverware. The food was arranged, and it looked more like a feast than a snack. "What is this?"

Meg smiled. "Honestly, we came by your house to kidnap you to bring you here. But you beat us to it. Of course, we were all going to get horses and ride out here, but since you had a head start, we didn't want to risk that you'd have left by the time we got here, so we drove."

Bella looked around at the women. "Why would you kidnap me?"

Tatum and Meg each took an arm, guiding her toward the picnic. "Eat and drink, my pretty," Meg teased. "So many questions from such a sweet little thing."

Bella pulled her arms free. "Look, I'm not going to be good company. I don't even want to be at the ranch—"

"That's why we're here." Meg sat down and so did the others, leaving Bella the only one standing.

She was so confused. "I don't understand what this is."

Meg looked at her, her cowboy hat casting shadows across her face. "When we were talking that night on the Cape before I left, and you made it so clear how you wanted to be away from the ranch, and wanted to be friends with those amazing women, it got me thinking."

Embarrassment flooded Bella's cheeks. "I didn't mean that you guys aren't amazing—"

Meg waved her off. "I know that, and that's what got me thinking. Our ranch used to be the boys and us, but now we have more women here. We're all pretty amazing, but the ranch is still kind of dominated by the boys. When I thought about it, I felt like we, as women, hadn't worked to build what we had. We weren't investing in *us*."

Bella blinked, surprised.

Phoebe raised her hand. "I'll admit that I would love to be more connected to you guys. I know I'm super busy helping Jacob become more comfortable with life, and I'm busy with my daughter and my coaching business, so I haven't been all that social as much either, but I would love for us to have some intentional girl time."

"Me, too," Sofia said. "I had some amazing friends in Seattle, and I miss them a lot. It's hard to build new friendships when you get older, and I've just focused my energy on Keegan, my stores, and my daughter, too. But I miss that level of comfort between women. I'd love for us to spend more time together."

"Me, too," Meg said.

Bella stood there, staring at these women. "Tatum, Sofia, and Phoebe," she began, her voice thick with emotion. "You all have these amazing accomplishments professionally. I felt like you would think I was just some rich girl with no purpose. And two of you are moms. What do I talk to you about? I don't know anything about being a mom or having a career. I didn't even really have a mom for long, and my only work is making food for a few dude ranch people and family."

Meg hopped up and put her arm around Bella's shoulders. "I love you, Bells."

Bella sighed. "I love you, too, Meg. I do. I just—"

"I know. You and I have always been alone in a sea of boys who like to protect us. You run the dude ranch kitchen by default, not because it was this great dream of yours. I want to do something more as well." She squeezed Bella's shoulder. "But we can grow together."

"I—" Bella spread her hands, unsure what to say.

It was Tatum who stood up. "Look, ladies, here we are. Five fantastic women who all live on the same ranch, part of the same family in different ways, and we have all made ourselves too busy and too insecure to invest in *us*." She turned to Bella. "I know we've never fully recovered from the damage I did to our trust when I left so long ago, but I'm tired of dancing around it and pretending that everything is as it was. I love you." She gestured to all of them. "I love each of you, and dammit, I claim you all as *mine*."

Sofia jumped to her feet. "I want to be claimed by you guys. I claim you back."

"Me too," Phoebe said. "Girl power matters, and we're forever girls, no matter how old we get."

Meg smiled at Bella. "What do you say, Bells? Do we expand our sisterhood with all of our heart?"

Bella took a breath, emotions clogging her throat. "I don't know how to let people in," she said. "I was hoping that Maddie and that gang would just suck me in so I wouldn't have to figure it out."

"We'll figure it out together," Phoebe said. "I don't know how anymore either."

"Me either," Meg said.

"I keep everyone at a distance," Tatum said. "The price of fame."

Sofia beamed at them. "I'm going to hold all of you to this," she said. "I'm great at having girlfriends, and I miss the hell out of it."

Bella started laughing through her sudden tears. "This is all just a ploy to keep me here, isn't it, Meg?"

Her sister kissed her cheek. "I'd never try to trap you, Bells, but I realized that we were missing out on something beautiful that was right here, waiting for us. You deserve it, even if you move away."

"We're all family," Tatum said. "All of us. Sisters." She slung her arm over Phoebe's shoulders. "Come on girls. Group hug. This is how it starts."

She flung her other arm around Sofia, and then Phoebe and Sofia held out their arms to Meg and Bella. Meg looked at her. "Bells?"

Bella nodded and walked over to the group. She barely got within reach when they dragged her in. They all lost their balance and almost fell down the rock, shrieking with laughter as they tried not to land in the water.

Bella leaned back on her hands, laughing as everyone straightened themselves out. "All right, Tatum, if we're friends now, how on earth did you become such an absolute badass with your career? How many Grammys now?"

"Eight." Tatum beamed at them. "Plus, I got two more nominations for this year."

Sofia grinned. "I'm literally ninety percent terrified of you, Tatum. You're a world-wide celebrity."

"Agreed," chimed in Phoebe. "I'm kind of afraid to talk to you at family events."

Tatum looked around, and Bella saw the sadness in her eyes. "You guys are afraid of me?"

"I'm not." Bella stood up, walked across the stone, and sat down next to Tatum. "I was mad at you, but I know you're the most beautiful soul. I've always loved you, Tatum."

Tatum put her arm around Bella. "Thanks, Bells. I love you, too, and I'm sorry I left."

"I know." Bella sighed. "I think part of the reason I was mad at you was because you had the courage to leave and go after your dreams, and I just stayed small and sat in the safe space that Brody created for me here on the ranch. It was about me." She glanced at Tatum. "Still is."

Tatum rested her hand on Bella's shoulder. "I'm going to write a song about female friendships," she said. "As women, we get so busy that we forget to invest in ourselves and in our connection to other women. And I want all of you in my video."

Sofia's face lit up. "No way! In your video! That's awesome. Yes!"

"Me, too," Phoebe said.

"I'm in," said Meg.

Bella hesitated. She'd worked so hard to stay hidden for so long, but if she were in Tatum's video, the whole world would see her. Was she ready for that?

Tatum frowned. "Not interested, Bella?"

She took a breath. "I have a stalker. A guy I dated a few years ago. He's—" She stopped.

"Psychotic," Meg said. "Creepy. Dangerous. All the things you think of. That's why Bella stays hidden. So he won't find her."

The three women looked startled. "I didn't know that," Tatum said. "Why didn't I know that?"

Bella shrugged. "My brothers scared him off. He'd never come after me here. But when I leave the ranch, he sometimes shows up. He knows where I go."

"Oh, damn." Phoebe looked worried. "I know what that's like. Don't be in the video."

Bella looked at Phoebe, who had gone into hiding to avoid her ex. "Is it worth it? To hide?"

Phoebe raised her brows. "I'm glad I'm not dead, so yes, I'd do it again."

Bella hugged her knees. She was sitting with two women who were so different. Tatum had gone into a life in the spotlight, not hiding. Instead, she had shined her own light so brightly, acquired more than one stalker, and had refused to back down.

Phoebe had gone into hiding for years, cutting off her own

family to escape her ex-husband, and then had done it a second time to protect her daughter.

Both women had ended up finding happiness and love. Family. Fulfillment. Careers that made them money and filled them with purpose and joy.

That meant either path could work.

So, what did Bella want to do?

"I want to shine my light," she said quietly.

"What?" Meg leaned in. "What did you say?"

Bella lifted her chin and looked around at the beautiful group of women surrounding her. "I want to shine my light," she said louder. "I think that's what I need. That's what's driving me to want to escape the ranch and the kitchen. I just want to no longer hide myself."

Tatum beamed at her. "Yes! So, you're in the video?"

Bella nodded. "I'm in." Screw her stalker. Let him come for her. She wasn't going to hide anymore.

"Whoohoo!" Tatum held up her arms. "I already thought of a few lines. You guys want to hear them?"

When everyone said yes, Tatum started to test out some lyrics, and soon they were in a creation hotspot, writing a song together about women.

Bella smiled as she listened to the conversation. These women, by marriage or by finding, were her family. Her sisters. All different, but all amazing people.

This is what she'd been missing. The power of women coming together, supporting each other, making each other laugh. And she'd had it all along. All of these women literally lived within walking distance of her house.

And she'd thought she had to run to Boston to find them.

Meg sat down next to Bella and nudged her shoulder. "Aside from the video, how are you going to shine your light, sis?"

"I don't know." She hugged her knees and rested her chin on them.

Tatum looked over. "What are you going to do about Falcon?"

Bella stiffened. "Nothing."

"Girl, he was sitting at the counter looking very distraught," Sofia said. "He looked like a man whose heart had just shattered. Did you dump him?"

Guilt flashed through Bella. "I didn't dump him. I just called his bluff, and he failed."

Meg raised her brows. "What bluff did you call?"

"I asked him to marry me, and he said he couldn't."

The women all screamed, and Meg hit her shoulder. "What are you talking about? Tell us *everything*."

Bella paused, looking around at all the women. She'd always been honest with Meg, but these other women? She wasn't used to that. She was used to not trusting. But these women had won over her brothers, and they were her family now. So, she took a deep breath, and she told them everything.

And it felt amazing.

It was when they started asking the tough questions that things got hard.

TWENTY-SEVEN

FALCON WAS STILL SITTING at the kitchen counter when the front door opened.

He looked over his shoulder, then turned when he saw it was Dylan and Brody. "Hey."

Both men nodded their greetings.

"Thanks for letting us know Bella took off," Brody said. "We tracked her and she's safe. The women are with her, and some of my brothers are hanging out, keeping watch."

Falcon nodded. Bella said he couldn't follow her, but he wasn't about to let her go out there unprotected. "I'm cancelling her request for you guys to take over the situation with the guy who attacked me on the Cape."

Dylan parked himself on the couch and put his feet up on a footrest. "No can do, buddy. You didn't hire me, so you can't fire me."

Falcon wasn't surprised by the response, but he tried again. "I'm not having someone endangered because of my shit. It's my job and I'll take care of it."

"How? By getting stabbed again?" Dylan grinned. "You did good. That guy was well-trained. He has a history. I'll

157

have no trouble tracking down his connection to you and Bella. It'll be over soon."

Falcon ground his jaw. "Dylan—"

"You realize that this shit you went through for twenty years could have been over a long time ago if you'd let us help?" Dylan leaned forward. "I know you decided not to be a Hart, but you're still one of us. No more of this crap of going alone, Falcon. It's bullshit, and it's over."

Falcon stared at him, surprised by the vehemence of his words.

Brody cleared his throat. "Here's the thing, Falcon. Man to man, I respect your need to live your life. But I heard the fear and pain in my sister's voice when you were passed out next to her, and she thought you were dying. Damn near broke my own heart. We've all been through too much to take on any pain we don't need. She deserves to be whole and loved. You say you love her, but you're going to ditch her and go get yourself killed?"

Guilt settled in Falcon's gut. "I didn't mean to scare her."

"But you did," Brody said. "And when Bella hired Dylan, it was to keep you alive, because she loves you. She knew you'd be pissed, and she said it would probably end the relationship, but she was doing it anyway."

"Yeah," Dylan added. "She said she'd rather have you alive and hating her than dead and loving her. That's love, my friend."

Those words settled deep in Falcon's gut.

Brody sat down on the end chair. "You broke through her defenses, Falcon, and that means you forfeited certain rights. You don't need to love her, but you don't get to be a dumbass who chases death because he has commitment issues."

Falcon blinked. "I don't have commitment issues." But as soon as he said it, he stopped. "Bella said I do," he admitted.

Brody smiled. "We all do, Falcon. When we come from such a fucked-up childhood, the shadows stay with us, until we decide to shine the light on them and make them dissolve. This is your chance. Shine the light or keep living in their grasp."

Falcon let out his breath and leaned back in his seat, clasping his hands on top of his head. "I don't think I'm good for her," he finally admitted.

"Why not?" Brody asked.

"We want different things. I don't want to trap her. She deserves her freedom."

Dylan snorted. "Are you so sure you'd be a trap?"

"Yeah, I want marriage and kids, and she doesn't—" He stopped himself as he said that. "Except she proposed to me. To test me."

The men exchanged glances. "You failed the test, I assume?" Dylan said. "That's why she left?"

"Yeah."

Silence fell in the house for a few minutes while the men let Falcon stew in his own thoughts.

"Bella wants you alive so much that she was willing to have you hate her forever. That's love," Brody finally said. "And you would rather get yourself killed than take away her dreams? That feels very similar. Deep love on both sides."

"Sure does," Dylan said. "Almost identical. Couple of idiots refusing to see what matters, you think?"

"There's a good chance of that," Brody said.

Falcon swiveled on the chair, suddenly restless. "Do you think," he asked slowly, choosing his words, "that I could be good for her? Be honest."

Brody grinned. "She loves you, and you love her. You're a good man, Falcon. You get us, and Bella, and our history, and you're so protective of her that it makes my big brother heart happy."

Falcon looked at Brody. "Do you think I'd make her *happy?*" He just wanted her happy. Whatever it took.

Brody looked at Dylan, then back at Falcon. "You two

are the ones who have to answer that. But answer it honestly, not influenced by the past that you both carry with you."

"That's impossible."

"It's not. You just have to shine your light brighter than the shadows to get started." Brody stood up. "Decide that you both have a right to be truly happy, and then see where that takes you." His hand knocked a notepad on the counter, and he glanced down at it, then smiled. "Read this note. She told us about you. And we support you fully."

"She told you what?"

But Brody was already headed toward the door.

Dylan launched himself to his feet. "The case isn't yours anymore, Falcon. Find something else to do with your life."

Then the two men let themselves out of the house, slamming the door behind them.

Falcon swore and leaned back in his seat. What the hell?

Find something else to do with his life.

Like what?

At that moment, his gaze fell upon the notepad. He recognized Bella's handwriting, and he saw the word "healer" jotted down. He grabbed the pad and pulled it over, scanning her notes with rising disbelief.

She had written down the names and phone numbers of three energy healers, and written a note to him.

Falcon, these are three top energy healers. I talked to each of them. They sound amazing. I pre-paid for a two-hour consult with each one. All you need to do is call them and set it up. You have a gift, and the world needs you. Love, Me.

Falcon's hands started shaking, and sudden emotion overtook him.

160

She truly believed in him and accepted him. And she'd told her family, and they felt the same.

He didn't have to hide it. Not from them.

Tears threatened, and he shoved them away.

He stood up and walked to the window, hands in his pockets as he gazed across the vast ranch that had called to him for so long. His people were here. His love was here.

This was where he wanted to be, not chasing some psycho across the globe for another twenty years.

Find something to do with your life.

He pulled his hands out of his pockets and looked down at them. They looked like normal hands. Nothing special.

But he turned his palms toward each other and imagined energy flowing between them.

In a moment, both his hands began to burn, and his fingers started tingling. The energy traveled up his arms, through his shoulders, down his sternum, and into his chest. He could feel the energy in his heart center vibrating, shaking, coming alive.

He wasn't imagining it. He knew he wasn't.

His gaze shifted to the notepad on the counter. What if he could make a difference for others? What if he did have the ability to somehow transmute the pain that echoed so rampantly through this world?

If there was any chance he could help, how could he say no, right?

He looked down at his hands, and sudden inspiration struck him. "Is my name Falcon?"

His hands moved further apart, of their own accord. *Yes.* The word was very clear in his mind, as if someone had spoken to him.

Excitement began to build inside him. "Is my name Bella?"

His hands moved closer together. *No.* Again, the word imprinted in his mind.

"Should I call those healers?"

His hands moved further apart. *Yes.*

He didn't ask again.

He simply walked across the room, pulled out his phone, and called the first number on the list.

When she answered, he said, "My name is Falcon, and I'm a healer."

TWENTY-EIGHT

THE WINE WAS GONE, the food had been reduced to a few crumbs, and Bella felt the happiest she'd felt in a long time.

Tatum was on her stomach, licking chocolate off her fingers, her feet crossed behind her. "I think Falcon's going to come after you," she said. "The man definitely loves you. He's just scared shitless."

"Like all the Harts are," Phoebe said. "Jacob was so fragile in some ways. Still is."

Bella inclined her head. "This is true."

"I was fragile too," Sofia chimed in. "I didn't want to get together with Keegan. But we healed each other."

Meg was leaning against a nearby rock. "Do you want him, Bella? For real? Do you really not want to get married and have kids?"

Bella rolled onto her back and stared at the sky, thinking about the question. "When I think of having kids, I think of all of us living under the bridge, carrying all this baggage. I have no idea how to be a good mom. I never saw it. I don't want to cause that damage to anyone. Ever."

Phoebe dipped a strawberry in the remnants of the chocolate. "I had a lot of trauma, and I'm figuring out how to be the mom my daughter needs. You don't need to be perfect. You just need to love them, and be who you are. You're amazing. It will be enough."

Sudden, surprising tears filled Bella's eyes. Was it really possible she could be enough? Deserving of a family? Capable of having a family? The notion that she might be enough was overwhelming, and suddenly she wanted to roll into a ball and cry. "I'm scared," she whispered. "So scared to believe in the fairytale."

"It's no fairytale," Tatum said. "It's real life. It's hard work. But it's worth it."

Bella turned her head to look at Tatum. "Are you happy with Brody?"

Her sister-in-law beamed at her. "Deliriously happy."

"What about your career?"

Tatum grinned. "Brody fully supports me and does everything he can to help me shine my brightest. He'd never hold me back. His support makes it easier for me to be successful, which means I work less. The Vegas residency allows me more time with him and at the ranch. He comes with me sometimes, and I come here. Between the two of us, we're together a lot, but we both have space to be ourselves. It works. It can work, Bella, if both sides are committed."

"Heck," Meg said. "Lucas moved to Boston to be with Maddie. I know they're back and forth from the ranch a lot, but he's having the best time out there. Our brothers raised us to be strong women, and they appreciate strong women. Falcon is the same. He'll support you in your career."

He would. Bella knew that.

"What do you want to do?" Phoebe asked. "Buy that catering business?"

Diana had called six times since they'd been talking, but

Bella hadn't answered. "I don't want to," she admitted. "I just don't know what else to do."

"Invest in their ice cream business, like you said," Sofia said.

Bella sighed. "I'm not interested in ice cream."

Meg raised her brows. "But are you interested in empowering women? Seeing them support each other?"

Bella glanced at her. "Well, yeah—"

"Do you know that some horrifyingly small percentage of venture capital money goes to women?" Tatum said. "Record companies are mostly owned by men. I started my own label last year, and I've taken on several artists."

Bella had heard the same speeches from Kitty, who had also opened her own label and invested regularly in women's businesses. "I don't know anything about business."

"Oh, well, that's a deal-breaker," Phoebe said sarcastically. "If only you could learn about it."

Bella grinned, recalling how she'd given Falcon that same speech about his healing. She thought about how happy Diana had been, calling her daughter to give her the news about the money so they could build her business.

At the very least, she could invest in their ice cream truck business, to make up for the fact she wasn't going to buy the catering company.

The minute she thought it, relief rushed through her. "I'm not buying it." The words felt amazing and free. "I'm not going to cook for the dude ranch either." She looked around. "I don't know if I want to be an investor, but I'll help with the ice cream trucks. Just to see—"

She paused when everyone looked past her, suddenly grinning.

Bella spun around, and her heart took a little leap when she saw Falcon astride their big, bay gelding, Moonstruck, reining the horse to a halt. He was wearing a cowboy hat and boots, and he looked every bit the rancher he wanted to be.

His shirt was open at the collar, and he looked so insanely sexy and at home.

God, she loved him.

"Hi," he said, his voice low and rough, his gaze only on her.

She lifted her chin. "I told you not to follow me."

"Yep, you did." He urged Moonstruck into a walk, and the pair sauntered into the clearing. He nodded at the others. "Hi, ladies."

They all waved, but none of them got up to leave. Bella realized they were staying with her, having her back, and her heart turned over. The day with these women had created a bond that was already taking root, real, deep roots of love.

Falcon reined Moonstruck to a halt, then swung his leg over and landed in front of Bella. He kept one hand on his horse's neck, scratching softly as he turned to Bella. "Thank you."

She shifted, restless. "For what?"

"For hiring Dylan."

Surprise stole her words for a moment. "Really?"

"Yes." He took a breath. "I had a good talk with Dylan and Brody. It's time to leave that behind."

Oh, thank God. Relief rushed through her. *Falcon wasn't going to get himself killed.* She nodded, her heart starting to race. "You didn't want to do it anyway," she said, trying to keep her voice calm.

"I didn't," he agreed, still scratching Moonstruck's neck. "And I called all three healers on your list. I've scheduled meetings with all of them."

Her throat suddenly clogged. "Really?"

He ground tied Moonstruck, then closed the distance between them. "If there is any chance I can make the world a better place, I have to do it. I'm going to try."

She nodded, emotions thick in her chest. "That's wonderful, Falcon."

He held out his hands to her, but she didn't take them. "You were right. I was scared of actually going after my dream." He didn't lower his hands. "I do want to get married to you, and only to you. Kids? Yeah."

She nodded, pressing her lips together.

"But I will tell you this," he said. "There are a lot of ways for me to help kids like we used to be. Like Gordy. If my healing works out, I'm going to find a way to help those kids. Do I want to be a dad? Yeah. But I don't need to be. You're my first and only, and if you don't want kids, I can make a hell of a lot of difference anyway."

Behind her, Bella heard the murmurs of her friends. Maybe some romantic sighs, which almost made her laugh.

"I do want to stay on the ranch, and I know you will always be connected here, too. We might find places we want to go, but our roots will always be here. I know it."

Bella nodded. "I know," she whispered. "I feel the pull of it when I'm here."

"Because it's built on love." He put his palm over her heart. "All I want is to heal this beautiful heart of yours and help it love."

He dropped to one knee, and tears filled Bella's eyes. "Bella Hart, I give you my whole heart. You've always had it. I want to marry you, and I'll never, ever break your trust. We will figure out how to thrive together, and it will be amazing."

She couldn't stop the tears now. "Falcon—"

"Hang on." He reached into his pocket and pulled out a little woven bag. "About ten years ago, I saw this ring. It spoke to me, and I knew it was for you. I've kept it on a chain around my neck every minute since then, except the last couple days, because I didn't want to freak you out."

She managed a giggle. "It would absolutely have freaked me out."

"Right? You're so predictable." He pressed the bag into

her hand, his hand warm and solid. "I kept you in my heart all this time, and this ring has years of love woven into it."

Behind her, the gallery was definitely making swooning sounds.

Bella opened the bag and slid the ring into her hand. "Oh," she whispered, stunned. "It's so beautiful." It was a huge center diamond with intricate carvings on the band and more diamonds woven into it, a pattern she'd never seen before. It was warm in her hand, and she closed her fist around it, absorbing the heat. "It's hot."

He nodded. "It's you. It's your energy and spirit. I knew it when I saw it." He held out his hand. "Marry me, Bella. It's been so long. No more waiting."

She smiled through her tears. This man, this beautiful man, had had her heart for years and years. He'd been her hero, and he'd let her grow into her own heroine as well. Time had made them both more, and they fit together now, better than when they were young. "I'm never going to let you be the boss. I've had enough protecting from my brothers."

He grinned. "I'm well aware of that, Bella. I love you as you are."

"I'm still figuring out my career."

"As I am," he said, hope building on his handsome face. "New identities for both of us."

She nodded. "Ask me again."

He grinned, took the ring from her, and then took her hand. "Bella Hart, will you marry me?"

She smiled as love filled her whole body. "Why, yes, Falcon. I will."

He let out a whoop, and she giggled as he slid the ring onto her finger. Then he swept her up in his arms and spun her around, whooping like a genuine cowboy. She wrapped her arms around his neck, laughing, her heart so full she felt like she was going to explode.

And when her friends, no, her *sisters*, came running over to bury them in hugs and shrieks, she knew that she'd found her home…right where it had been all along.

TWENTY-NINE

"GIRLFRIEND, you are amazing! What is this magic?" Tatum exclaimed, holding up her spoon.

Bella grinned. "It's called Sassy Lassy. It's good, right?"

"Freaking amazing!" Tatum looked over at Meg, Maddie, Sofia, and Phoebe, who were all sampling the same flavor. "I can't believe you're an ice cream maven, now."

"I know, right?" Bella grinned. "I had no idea how much fun it would be to create new flavors of ice cream. It's actually so complicated to get it right. And now that we're selling the vegan line too, it's very challenging. I love it."

Meg raised her brows. "How much did you make this year in your gourmet ice cream business?"

Bella grinned. "We just hit eight figures for the year. We added ten trucks in three cities, and I've picked up a couple huge retail accounts."

"You're a marketing genius," Tatum said. "I'm going to have to hire you away from yourself."

Bella laughed. "No way. I love this."

Sofia waved her spoon. "And to think you invested because you felt bad about pulling out of the catering gig. Just goes to show you never know where life leads you."

"And then you went and bought the catering business anyway," Meg said, "when Diana was reluctant to walk away from her legacy. You've made such a difference to LaToya and all the women she has hired to run it. Complete empowerment and opportunity for underrepresented women."

Joy flooded Bella. LaToya Johnson had been working at a crappy restaurant, a single mom without the resources to get out and start her own business. When Bella had found her and hired her, LaToya had fully staffed the entire catering business with underrepresented women, all of whom had had a tough break in life and needed a chance that no one else would give them.

Bella was proud to be a part of that movement, and she'd started looking for more opportunities to reach out into communities to help talented, underrepresented women who were ready to flourish with just a little bit of help.

But the ice cream business filled her creative side like her soul needed. "I got lucky. Diana and Jessie are smart and amazing, and they were the right people to grow the ice cream business. When I suggested we make our own gourmet ice cream, that changed everything." She held her hand out toward her friends. "And I have to thank you guys for always coming over here and trying my new flavors. You've made a big difference."

Tatum took another scoop. "You guys help me with my songs, too. My new album has a release date. Next month, on the fifteenth."

"What?" Bella shrieked, and everyone cheered. "What did you call it?"

Tatum looked pleased. "*Her*."

"Oh my God, that's so perfect," Sofia said. "An entire album focused on the power of women. No one does that. Literally no one."

"Well, I'm at the top of the food chain in the music industry, so I can do whatever I want," Tatum said with a wink.

"And I want little girls all over the world to listen to the lyrics and feel like they can be strong, powerful, and create whatever life they want, no matter what."

"Amen to that, sister." Phoebe raised her glass. "The women in my confidence program are going to freak out when they find out you're doing a class on unleashing your inner badass."

"I'm very expensive," Tatum said. "Don't forget you'll owe me a free lunch by Hart Pond."

Bella grinned. "God, I love you guys. I never thought I'd feel so happy and comfortable with you all, but it's amazing what has happened in a year, isn't it?" It had taken only a few weeks for Dylan and his team to solve the situation with the man who had tracked them to Cape Cod. It turned out, it had been a man who was owed money by Falcon's biological father, and he'd decided to try to get the money from the Harts. Simple, clean, and easy to unpack.

Bella's stalker had found her one evening when she'd been doing a photoshoot in LA. And for the first time in her life, she'd stood up for herself with her voice, and using some of her magical self-defense skills, with Falcon looming over the situation looking quite monster-ish.

Her stalker had wound up needing stitches and a cast. He'd never bothered her again, and she'd spent weeks feeling like a goddess. Still kinda did, actually.

Phoebe leaned forward. "Is Falcon around this weekend?"

Bella nodded. "He's due back any minute. He went for a ride. Why?"

"The healing he did with Annie a few days ago made such a difference. I know he releases trauma that is stored as energy blocks, but I still find it amazing. I'm also like a different person. Even Jacob noticed, and he's decided to work with Falcon."

"And my hands—" Tatum held up her hand and wiggled

her fingers. "For years, I've had stiffness in them, and they're completely fine."

Bella smiled, immense satisfaction spreading through her. "He's going out to Sedona next week for a five-day intensive on physical healing. He's so passionate and so talented."

Meg sighed. "It's so amazing how both of you have lit up since finding each other and your passions. I'm not going to lie, I'm massively jealous of all of you. I feel like I'm still floundering. Don't get me wrong, I love using my financial wizardry as your ice cream CFO, but it's your business, not mine."

Bella put her arm around her sister and gave her a quick hug. "You'll find your place, Meg. I didn't think I would, but I did."

Meg nodded. "I know. You inspire me." She grinned at them. "You guys all inspire me. You've all found your career passion and love, so it's my turn."

Tatum smiled warmly. "It'll be your turn when you're ready. You ready?"

Meg looked around at them all. "I think I might be."

They all cheered and pulled Meg into a laughing hug. God, Bella was so happy. She never knew she could be so happy—

The front door suddenly opened, and she looked over as Falcon walked in the door. He was dusty from his ride, looking rough and rugged and extremely delicious. He'd discovered he liked being clean-shaven, and he looked so much younger without the scruffy beard. His cowboy hat was tipped back so she could see his beautiful face, and he flashed her that smile that made his eyes crinkle up with laughter.

God, he looked happy. Relaxed. Carefree.

She knew it was because he was living his purpose work, the life he was meant to live, and she was so lucky that it included her. "Hey there, gorgeous," she said.

He blew her a kiss, his wedding ring catching the light coming in through her picture windows. The wedding ring they'd picked out together. "Sassy Lassy a hit?" he asked, aware that today had been a final tasting of the new flavor.

"Of course," Tatum said. "Your wife is a genius."

"I know." Pride was evident on his face and in his voice, and Bella's heart expanded. "She's incredible. I fall more in love with her every day."

"Aww..." Meg put her hand over her heart. "You guys are literally the sweetest---"

"Mommy! Mommy! I galloped today! I galloped on Night Blade!" Gordy came running in behind Falcon, his little cowboy hat askew, and his red cowboy boots finally covered in dirt, after months of Gordy being afraid to get them dirty, because they were the best thing he'd ever had in his life.

"Wow! I'm so proud of you!" Bella crouched down, catching Gordy as he flung himself into her arms. She stood up, propping him on her hip as he filled her in on all the details of his trip.

His brown eyes were twinkling with joy, making her heart dance. "Daddy said today was the day. Is it really today?"

She grinned and looked at Falcon. "Is it today?"

He nodded. "Yep."

"Today! Today!" Gordy bounced in her arms, then wiggled to get down. "I made her a bed. I'll go get it." He sprinted up the stairs, his little feet pounding.

Meg raised her brows. "What's today?"

Bella looked at Falcon and smiled. "Today's the day we're picking our new dog."

"A new dog? You're getting a dog?" Phoebe grinned. "Cupcake will be so happy to have another dog on the ranch! What is the dog like?"

"A three-legged, eighty-pound pit bull," Falcon said.

"Named Athena," Bella added. "She was rescued from a

terrible situation, and it took her foster mom months to build her confidence back up. She was forty pounds when they took her in."

"Oh…" Meg put her hand over her heart. "And now she has you guys."

Bella nodded, smiling as Falcon walked up, put his arm around her waist, and kissed her cheek. "Gordy picked her, but we all felt the bond with her. She's going to learn to feel safe again."

"And love," Falcon said. "She'll get to know what it feels like to be loved."

Bella smiled at him. "Always loved. By all of us."

Falcon's smile was just for her. "Always loved, Bells. *Always.*"

Things get sassy and spicy in *When We Least Expect It!* If you can't stand the heat, get out of the wedding! Except that the chemistry between wedding planner Piper Townsend and her fake fiancé, ex-cop Declan Jones, is scorching hot…and in danger of combusting into something more real than either of them wants. Sparks fly when the sassy runaway bride recruits her reclusive landlord into her world of romance, tuxedoes, and happily-ever-after when she and Declan make a deal to fake an engagement for twenty-one scorching hot days. Treat yourself to *When We Least Expect It* today or keep reading for a sneak peek!

CHAPTER ONE

THERE WAS A SHIRTLESS, MUSCLED MAN in Piper Townsend's shower, and that was just not going to work for her today.

Or ever, quite honestly.

But especially today.

She put her hands on her hips as her landlord, Declan Jones, reared back with a freaking sledgehammer and aimed it at her still-intact shower wall. "Declan, don't—"

Her grumpy, ex-cop demolition squad slammed his sledgehammer into the tile, shattering the wall and eviscerating the last vestiges of composure she'd been clinging to when she'd walked in.

"Declan!" She strode into the bathroom and poked him in his shoulder.

He spun around so fast that he bumped into her, knocking her off balance. She tripped on his toolbox, and he grabbed her arm, swearing as he averted her certain death and hauled her upright again.

Of course he could toss her effortlessly to her feet. That was so irritatingly attractive in a man, and she didn't have time for irritatingly attractive men.

He pulled his earbuds out and scowled at her. "Don't sneak up on me when I have a sledgehammer. It's not safe."

"I literally shouted your name twice."

He frowned. "You did?"

She pointed to his earbuds. "Noise-cancelling?"

He looked down at his hand, then swore. "Sorry." He shoved the earbuds in his pocket. "You okay?"

Okay was such a vague term. "Technically, yes."

His brows went up. "You're not okay?"

"You didn't hurt me," she clarified, because did she want to have to explain to him what had happened to her in the last twenty-four hours? No, she didn't. Home was her oasis, and Declan was probably the only human within a few hundred miles who didn't know what had happened.

Or maybe that was an exaggeration, but that's what it felt like, so she was going with it.

"All right." He picked up the sledgehammer. "What do you need?"

"My bathroom, but that feels like a reach right now." Normally, a glimpse of Declan's gorgeous shoulders was enough to boost Piper's mood in an art-appreciation kind of way, but today his royal hotness was simply a big mass of muscles and man in her way. She did not have time for her bathroom to be in a pile of rubble.

Declan glanced over at her with those bright blue eyes that always startled her with their intensity. "I told you I was starting the renovation today." He sounded cranky and tired.

Well, that was great for him that he was cranky and tired. So was she, and it was her bathroom that he'd just punctured a hole in. "Wednesday. You said you were starting Wednesday."

He frowned. "I said today."

"No, you said that you had to finish the molding in your kitchen, so you weren't going to start until Wednesday." It was currently Monday afternoon at five, which was not the time for Declan to be in her shower.

Well, in an alternate life, maybe any time would be the perfect time for Declan to be in her shower, but in this life? Never.

He narrowed his eyes, staring at her.

"Hello?"

"I think I did say Wednesday," he finally said.

Piper blinked. "I don't think I've ever heard you admit you were wrong about anything."

He flashed her a grin as he rested the sledgehammer against his leg. "I'm not that stubborn."

"You are, but I'm used to it." She waved her hand at her bathroom. "But about this—"

He'd offered to pay for a hotel while he redid her bathroom, but this was her oasis, and she'd needed the comfort of being there. She had a tiny powder room that had a toilet and a sink, and she could shower at her gym, so she'd decided it would work. "I didn't plan for this tonight. I need a shower."

And a miracle, but first things first.

Declan sighed and ran his hand over his short hair, his chiseled bicep flexing like God's gift to women. His hotness had never dawned on her prior to the last few weeks, but her trio of besties had recently been on a mission to get Piper back into the dating game, and they'd fixated on Declan as a good start.

She disagreed, but their constant harping on his physical attributes was working its way into her subconscious, which was incredibly distracting and annoying, especially when he was shirtless and sweaty.

Fortunately, she had a will of steel and enough relationship trauma to withstand any temptation, so it was all good.

"It was my mistake," Declan said, "so you can shower at my place."

"Your place?" Piper had never been in his gorgeous house that shared a gravel driveway with her little carriage house. She'd never even peeked through those beautiful French doors or tiptoed past his gorgeous, landscaped pool. Declan was private, closed-off. Almost a loner, from what she'd observed from her little vantage point in his guest house. He kept people away, except for the occasional visit by his parents, brother, and sister, whom she'd met a couple times.

Declan was a reclusive ex-cop who spent his life in jeans, boots, T-shirts, and a five o'clock shadow. His sole existence appeared to be working on his house, playing ball with his dog, and bartending part-time at a neighborhood bar.

His family was well-dressed, sociable, and always looked like they knew what a shower was for. She had no idea how they were related.

"Yeah. Back door is unlocked." Declan looked at his watch. "I'll be working until six, so you'll have privacy. Use the guest bath to the left at the top of the stairs. It's the blue bathroom."

Piper stared at him. "You're inviting me unattended into your sanctuary?"

He cocked a brow. "Why? Should I not trust you?"

"No. I'm very trustworthy." Well, apparently she was also demon spawn cursed to destroy love and romance in all its earthly forms, but she doubted Declan would be worried about that apparent flaw in her character. He didn't seem the type.

He grinned. "I know you're trustworthy. I ran a background check on you before I rented you the carriage house. You have an hour. Once I'm finished in here for the night, I'm kicking you out, so make it quick."

A background check? Sudden alarm gripped her. Did he know about her past? He was an ex-cop. If he'd decided to dig deep, his tentacles would have gone far. "What did you check?"

His smile faded. "Credit. Prison record."

"That's it?"

He leaned on his sledgehammer, studying her with open curiosity now. "What else is there to find, Piper?"

"Nothing." She shook out her shoulders. If Declan had uncovered her past, he wouldn't have rented her the carriage house. It was fine. Her past was still hidden. No one except her friend Maddie Vale knew. Relax, Piper. She ducked past him and grabbed her shampoo and conditioner off the sink where he'd moved it. "I'll be on my way—"

"You getting married?" he asked.

"What?" Alarm leapt through her, then she saw he was looking toward her left hand. Where there was no longer an engagement ring. Had he heard what happened?

He pointed. "The magazine."

She looked down and saw that her copy of the June issue of Elite Bride was facing him. Relief rushed through her. He didn't know. "No. I'm a wedding planner."

Or rather, a wedding killer, according to Kathryn Vespa, one of her bridal clients.

Kathryn had also called her cursed.

And bad luck.

And, most significantly, fired.

A second bride had also fired her today. And social media had embraced the new, viral hashtag #weddingkillerpiper.

And a third bride, the biggest client her firm had ever acquired, had left Piper three voicemails today, demanding that Piper call her back. She wasn't going to do that until she figured things out, since bride #3, April Hunsaker, was definitely going to fire her.

April was her last chance. If April fired her, Piper's career would be over.

Everything she'd worked for…destroyed.

Which meant she had to figure out how to regain April's trust tonight.

As in, within the next few hours.

Tomorrow, it would be too late.

Game over.

Piper had twelve hours to fix the unfixable. Hence the need for a miracle.

She'd find a way, but right now, she had no idea what that path was. She was worried that there wasn't an out, and that scared her more than she wanted to admit.

"Wedding planner?" Declan looked amused. "That job title brings fear into every man's heart."

"What? Why? I make dreams come true. And very well, I might add." Well, except for the string of bad luck over the last ten months…beginning with her own. But that wasn't bad luck so much as a nightmare of her own creating. Either way, same result, though.

"The bride's dreams, maybe, but that poor groom?" Declan chuckled. "Now he's got two women to complicate his life. All he wants is to get married, and now he has to deal with things like tablecloths, seating charts, and table centerpieces."

Piper rolled her eyes. "That's so unromantic! Just wait until you fall in love. You'll realize that your greatest joy is seeing your bride's face light up as her dream day comes to life."

His amusement faded, and his jaw got hard. "No chance. No wedding in my future."

It was her turn to be curious. His reaction had been intense and unyielding, far beyond a typical marriage-averse manly-man reaction. "Really? Why not?"

Something flashed across Declan's face, an emotion so raw and ragged that she sucked in her breath. "Because it's not." He turned away, picked up his construction assault weapon, and slammed it into the wall of her shower again.

Piper didn't move for a moment, stunned by the expression she'd seen on his face. Declan was always so reserved, so controlled, so grumpy, but that had been pure, raw emotion raking across his face for that brief second.

Declan had secrets, she realized. Secrets that would probably rip him to shreds if he let them out.

Wow. Just...wow. She'd had no idea that her reserved, solitary landlord was a boiling cauldron of secrets.

He looked over his shoulder at her. "You're down to fifty-eight minutes."

"Right. I'm going." She grabbed the rest of her toiletries and bolted.

Declan had just gone from annoyingly attractive on a physical level to maddeningly intriguing on an human level.

Which didn't fit into her life.

At all.

Piper was standing on the ruins of a promise she'd made to her mother before she'd passed away. If she failed to fix things in the next twelve hours, the dream she and her mom had created together would be shattered.

She needed miracles right now, not mistakes.

And Declan would be a mistake.

A huge, irrecoverable mistake.

Which meant she was keeping her distance from him.

In every way.

Because she was a woman on a mission, and she wasn't going to mess it up with romantic dreams of knights in shining armor.

She'd done that twice already, and the scars still burned.

Never, ever again.

Declan could still smell the flowers.

Piper was gone, and yet, he could still smell the flowers. Was it her shampoo? Her soap? Some sort of body lotion?

The thought of body lotion put a visual in his head that made him swear.

He set his sledgehammer down and stepped back, trying to focus on the carnage around him. Demolition was always satisfying. He knew damn well that he'd told Piper he was starting on Wednesday, but a few hours ago, he'd run into someone he used to know, and his past had been triggered.

He'd had to do something to distract himself. From the memories. From the pain in his gut. From the truth that wouldn't stop haunting him.

Declan had grabbed his tools and almost sprinted to the guest house, ignoring the instability in his knee. That first swing of the sledgehammer had reverberated through his body, jerking him back from the grips of the past and returning him to the present.

Now? He felt back in control again, locked down, focused...except for the fact he could still smell the scent of flowers that seemed to follow Piper wherever she went.

He fucking loved how she smelled.

He was going to have to find a way to get over it.

Because he wasn't ready for a woman, and he never would be.

That part of his life was over, and he was never going back.

At that moment, his phone rang. He pulled it out and looked at the caller. When he saw who it was, he had to take a breath before answering it. "Declan here."

He listened for a moment, his gut tightening the longer they spoke. "Yeah, I can come in on Friday at eleven. Thanks."

He hung up and let his hand fall to his side, stunned.

He'd passed the physical to return to police work.

Interview on Friday.

After three years on the sidelines, fighting to get his body to work again, he'd done it.

It was all he'd been focused on. The only thing that mattered.

But now that he was going back there on Friday... Fuck.

It was only for an interview, but the nightmares were going to start again. He could already feel it.

He took a breath. Nightmares were fine. He was fine. He had a bathroom to destroy and that would get him right.

But as he picked up the sledgehammer, he caught a whiff of flowers again.

This time, he closed his eyes, paused, and inhaled, using that light, delicate scent to steady himself.

Piper was freaking sunshine, and she had no idea how she grounded him every time he saw her.

And she never would know, because he was never going there with her.

But would he take a minute to breathe in the flowers and let it settle him?

Yeah. He would.

Because he had only a few days to figure out how to make himself walk back into that station, and the life that had nearly destroyed him.

Want to read more? Get When We Least Expect It now!

~

Want to know when Stephanie's next book is coming out, or when she's having a sale? Join her newsletter at www. stephanierowe.com.

~

Check out Stephanie's other series below, or keep scrolling for free excerpts of other Stephanie Rowe books!

. . .

What about heart-melting, fun, small-town romance? A new *Birch Crossing* **is available!** Leila Kerrigan is back in town with no time for the rebel who stole her heart long ago...but now he's playing for keeps. Treat yourself to *Secretly Mine* today or skip ahead to a sneak peek! It's a connected stand-alone, so you can enjoy it without reading any of the other *Birch Crossing* books (but you'll probably want to go back and read the others when you're done)!

New to Stephanie's cowboy world, and want more heart-melting cowboys? If so, you *have* to try her *Wyoming Rebels* series about nine cowboy brothers who find love in the most romantic, most heartwarming, most sigh-worthy ways you can imagine. Get started with *A Real Cowboy Never Says No* right now. You will be sooo glad you did, I promise!

If you want more small-town, emotional feel-good romances like the *Hart Ranch Billionaires*, you'd love my *Birch Crossing* series! Get started with *Unexpectedly Mine* today! Or jump in with the brand-new Birch Crossing book, *Secretly Mine*, or skip ahead to a sneak peek.

Are you in the mood for some feel-good, cozy mystery fun that's chock full of murder, mayhem, and women you'll wish were your best friends? If so, you'll fall in love with *Double Twist!*

Are you a fan of magic, love, and laughter? If so, dive into my paranormal romantic comedy *Immortally Sexy* series, starting with the first book, *To Date an Immortal.*

· · ·

Is dark, steamy paranormal romance your jam? If so, definitely try my award-winning *Order of the Blade* series, starting with book one, *Darkness Awakened.*

Keep scrolling for sneak peeks of Stephanie Rowe books! You might find your next binge-read right here!

SNEAK PEEK: TRIPLE TROUBLE

A MIA MURPHY MYSTERY

"So much darn fun!" Five-star Goodreads Review
(Penny)

CHAPTER ONE

X.

I stared at my phone, stunned at the text that had just come in from an unfamiliar number. My brain immediately shouted at me that the X meant bad things, bad, bad things.

Then I remembered that I wasn't ten years old in the middle of a con with my mom. She wasn't standing on the other side of a luxurious room crowded with celebrities, holding up two crossed fingers, giving me the X sign that meant "abandon the con right now because it's going south."

I was, in fact, a grown woman who had walked away from that life and my mom ten years ago. I was currently standing on my dock in the gorgeous morning sunlight on a beautiful Maine lake, going over my list of all the must-do items still undone prior to the grand reopening of my new marina.

Not a celebrity or con in sight. And definitely no mom.

I took a breath. Wow. My head had gone to old places in an alarming hurry.

I grinned at my massive rescue cat, who was perched on the end of the dock, his tail twitching in anticipation of the next unsuspecting fish to swim past. "It's all good, King Tut."

He ignored me, but I knew that the love was still there.

My life was great. I had friends, a home, and a marina that I was determined to turn into a success. I looked down at my phone again, studying my list. The landscapers were due to finish today, and—

A second X popped up.

My heart sped up, and I sucked in my breath. *What the fudge?*

Tentatively, almost terrified of getting a response, I texted back. *Mom?*

I got an immediate, automated reply stating that the phone number was not in service.

I felt both relieved and weirdly sad. Of course it wouldn't be my mom. I hadn't had any contact with her since I'd left her when I was seventeen. Granted, I'd always felt that she knew exactly where I was and what I was doing, but even if that were true, why would she be texting me *XX* after all these years?

One X had meant abandon the con. XX had meant that it was getting dangerous and to get out as soon as possible. Get out? From my own home? That made no sense. But I couldn't help but take a more careful look around me.

The lake was relatively quiet, but there were a few boats around. Across the cove was Jake's Yacht Club, with its upscale blue and white awnings. Staff in their navy shirts and khaki shorts were strolling around helping customers. Everyone was calm. No danger that I could see.

I studied each driver of the boats that were near me, but I recognized everyone. No one new.

I turned around to examine my marina. The painters were working, the landscapers were making things beautiful. The front window that had been shot out my first week, almost killing one of my new besties, had been replaced, so the big plywood board was gone.

Everything was coming along well.

But despite all the warm fuzzies surrounding me, I could feel panic starting to build in my chest. I'd been relaxed for days, so the sudden descent into panic was throwing me. I was out of practice being on guard for my life.

I looked at King Tut again. He was my gold-star surveillance system. He'd sacrificed morals, pride, and common decency to save me more than once. "King Tut!"

He didn't take his gaze off the lake.

I took a breath, trying to get my head back into focus. The fact King Tut wasn't concerned meant there wasn't a threat. Granted, it could also mean that he was so deeply immersed in predator mode that he had no mental space for anything else…

My phone dinged again. My heart jumped, and I looked down.

X.

Three Xs.

Three Xs meant *get out fast, no matter what it takes.*

I looked around again, the hair on the back of my neck prickling even as I tried to talk myself out of freaking out. It was a few Xs. There was nothing special about an X. Anyone could type an X. Glitches could produce Xs with zero effort.

I was at home at my marina. What could possibly be so dangerous that I needed to get out as fast as I could? My mom's messes hadn't been mine for a very long time.

Then my gaze settled on Vinnie, the sometime-gang-leader-ish guy who was currently acting as my unofficial bodyguard, due to the fact that my real one had been murdered (by a person unrelated to me and my life). The feds still couldn't figure out who had put surveillance cameras in my marina, so Vinnie had taken over keep-Mia-alive duty.

It had never once occurred to me that the spying had anything to do with my mother. I'd assumed it was connected to my ex-husband, who was currently in federal prison for being a drug kingpin. I'd put him there, and his mom had tried to kill me for it.

Vinnie was standing in the parking lot, his arms folded as he scanned the area. He looked dangerous and armed, despite the fact he had already admitted he would never shoot anyone for me, due to his aversion to a life of guilt and trauma, and things like that.

But at six-foot four, muscular, and wearing just the right amount of bling for a gang leader, he looked like a deadly force, so I doubted anyone would try while he was around. Plus, honestly, after spending so long looking over my shoulder, I'd gotten used to the possibility of being a target.

I was chill now.

Except, apparently, when being triggered by my past.

I looked down at my phone again, trying to think of a reply that might help me figure out if the sender was my mom.

My mom had been a code person, because living a life of crime had taught her that paper trails were never good for the criminal.

I tried to remember something from the code we'd used,

but all I could think of were the made-up symbols that we'd created, none of which were on the keyboard of my phone (go figure, right?). I couldn't quite recall how any of them went together anyway.

I did remember the symbol for my name, though.

I quickly knelt on the dock, dipped my finger in the water, and then drew the symbol on the wood. I took a picture of it then texted it to the number.

Again, an immediate reply that the number was not in service.

Then, right after that, another text came through. *XXX*.

Alarm shot through me, the kind that she'd triggered in me so many times as a kid. *Run, Mia, run!*

"King Tut," I shouted. "Let's go. Now." I didn't know where to go, but I had to get out, and get out fast. I had no idea what was happening, but I liked my life too much to be willing to die. "Vinnie," I shouted. "We gotta go!"

Vinnie started running toward me, but King Tut ignored me. I ran to the edge of the dock to get him. Leaving my cat behind didn't qualify as "no matter what." He was my family, and there was no way I was leaving him. "King Tut! We gotta go—"

He shot off the dock and dove into the water, disappearing under the surface. "Hey!"

I immediately jumped in after him, knowing that sometimes King Tut vanished for hours once he got under the water. I didn't know where he went, but wherever he came up for air was out of my sight. It used to freak me out, but I'd gotten used to it.

But now was not the time to lose my cat for hours. The late June water was warming, but still a shock to my system as I hit the lake. I immediately ducked under, searching the crystalline water for my black cat.

I didn't see him.

I stood up, water dripping off me. Vinnie was already at the end of the dock. "What's happening?" He looked alarmed.

"Where's King Tut? Can you see him? We need to get out of here, but I need to get him first!"

"King Tut?" Vinnie pulled off his sunglasses and scanned the water.

At that moment, I heard the roar of the lake patrol boat. I whirled around and waved my hands at Devlin Hunt, the too-handsome-for-anyone's-good cop who was driving it. "Stop!" I shouted. "King Tut's under the water! Turn off your propeller!"

Because we'd done this drill many times since I'd bought the marina a few months ago and discovered that my cat was an avid underwater hunter, Devlin immediately shut his boat off and leaned over the edge to search the water.

For a long moment, there was silence as the three of us scanned the water for my baby.

"There!" Devlin pointed close to the beach, and I sloshed through the water toward where he was pointing, my heart pounding.

"Something's wrong!" I shouted as I hurried after King Tut. "I'm in danger!"

"What?" Devlin stood up and put his hand on his gun. "What's going on?"

"I don't know!" I saw a black shadow under the water, and I lunged for him. My hands wrapped around King Tut's waist, and I dragged the yowling beast out of the water. "I need to go!" I started running toward the shore. I had no idea what the danger was or where it was coming from, which made me even more alarmed.

Just as I reached the shore, fighting to hold into a sodden ball of long-haired anger, an extended-cab pickup truck shot into the parking lot. I knew that black truck. It belonged to one of my two best friends, Hattie Lawless, a seventy-some-

192

thing chef who ran a café in my marina and raced cars on the side. "Hattie!"

She hit the brakes and the truck skidded to a stop. She jumped out, grabbing my shoulders as I ran up. "What's going on? Why do you look like you're freaking out?"

"A triple X! I think my mom sent me a triple X!"

"Is that porn?" Hattie looked intrigued. "I had no idea your mom was into porn. I mean, not surprising because she's a wild card, but porn? Can I see it? I assume it's girl power porn, right? She seems empowered."

"Porn?" I stared at her. "No. It's our signal that the con has gone south, and we need to run."

"A con?" Her eyebrows shot up. "You're running a con with your mom? What con?"

"I'm not. I mean, that I know of. But I got this text from this random number, and it could have been her, and—"

"Wait a minute." Hattie put her hands on her hips. "Mia Murphy. Pull yourself together. You're not running a con. You own a marina in the charming town of Bass Derby. You don't engage in illegal activities, except to help others. And you haven't heard from your mom in over a decade. Whatever you think is going on, isn't."

I grabbed my phone and handed it to her as Vinnie ran up. "See?"

Hattie took the phone, and the two of them peered at it. "This?" Hattie frowned at me. "Some random text from a number that doesn't even work? You're freaking out about *this?* How do you know it's her?"

"I don't *know* it's her, but what if it is? What if there's something going on and she's trying to warn me and—"

"Hey!" Hattie cut me off. "Take a breath, girlfriend." She held up her hands palm up and inhaled. "Deep breath. Channel your inner river."

I blinked. "My river?"

"Yes. A calm, scenic river. Tranquility. Peace. Serenity.

Imagine chiseled, charming men lined up on the banks, singing about how wonderful you are."

I stared at her. "Seriously?"

"Yes. Imagine their deep voices, singing 'Mia is a badass. She rules the world!' Maybe they're even dancing for you, some manly, synchronized beauty. How can that not feel good? Breathe in. Breathe out."

Devlin finally caught up to us. "What's going on?"

"Keep channeling your river, Mia. I got this." Hattie held up my phone. "Mia thinks this text is from her mom, signaling that the end of the world is upon us, and she must run away. To where? She doesn't know. From what? Also unknown."

Devlin took the phone and frowned at it. As he studied it, I found my pulse slowing and my panic easing. Devlin was a local cop in the small town of Bass Derby, but I was pretty certain he had a black ops background.

His buddy, Agent Hawk Straus, who I called Griselda to reclaim my personal power, was the FBI agent who had coerced me into a two-year-undercover sting against my ex. When I'd moved to Bass Derby, Griselda had asked Devlin to make sure no one from my ex's life assassinated me. He trusted Devlin with my life, which means I did, too. With Devlin standing by my side, no one would be able to get to me.

Plus, the river visualization had been surprisingly helpful.

I took the deep breath Hattie had wanted for me, and she nodded her approval as she studied me. "It's not like you to freak out like that," she observed. "You're very unflappable when it comes to danger like assassins, guns, and other immi-nent threats to your life. Why are you having a fit over this?"

Devlin looked over at me. "Hattie's right. This could easily just be some random text."

They were right. I usually was pretty calm. A childhood of crime had inured me to the small dangers in life. In fact, it had instilled in me an affinity for a high-risk life, which I tried to suppress as much as possible. "I know. It's just…well…it's my *mom*."

"It's probably *not* your mom," Hattie said.

"I know. I just meant that she triggers me." I let out my breath again. "The purpose of the triple X code was to get my attention when I wasn't taking things seriously. She would use it to freak me out and get me to do what she needed me to."

Hattie cocked her brow. "That sounds a little manipulative."

"When you're a criminal, sometimes you can't mess around." I looked over at Devlin, who was frowning at me. "What?"

He held up my phone. "I'm going to have Griselda, I mean Hawk, track this number and see what he can figure out."

I nodded. "Okay, great. Thanks."

"But in the meantime, I agree with Hattie," he said. "Keep an eye out, but we're already on alert, so I don't think we raise the alarm any higher. Unless you know something else?"

I looked at the three of them, and buried my chin in King Tut's soggy head. "You know, I think you guys are right. It makes no sense that my mom would be telling me to run from here." My tension eased even more. "It was an old trigger, I guess."

"We all have those," Devlin said softly.

I knew he understood. He'd been in a gang when he was a kid, so I imagined he had his own share of childhood land mines that came up from time to time. "Thanks."

He nodded. "It's all good, Mia." But he continued to study me. "You do look like hell, though."

"Thanks." Not too long ago, Devlin had declared his interest in dating me. On the same day, Griselda had made the same announcement. They were besties. Griselda had warned me off Devlin. Devlin had warned me off Griselda. I didn't want to ever date anyone again.

It was awkward.

And yet somehow, I'd agreed to have dinner with Devlin tomorrow night. Umm…

Hattie peered at me. "You know, you do look haggard. It can't all be from that text."

"Mia was up all night working on the marina," Vinnie offered. "She's freaking out about having it ready in time for her grand reopening."

Empathy flashed across Hattie's face. "Sweetie, it looks amazing. It's going great."

"I know, but it's just that I have to overcome the marina's reputation and mine. Do you know that the sheriff came over here with some woman a couple days ago? She'd lost her diamond ring and accused me of taking it, due to my criminal history and all."

Devlin narrowed his eyes. "I didn't know about that." No one in the entire town was impressed with our sheriff, not even the mayor, who had hired him. She also happened to be his mom.

"Well, the lady found it under her own bed," I said.

"Which you could have put there," Hattie said. "It doesn't exonerate you."

I looked at her. "How is that helpful?"

"Just wanted to remind you of your awesomeness. Just because someone doesn't appreciate your specialness or sees it as a threat doesn't make you any less awesome." She put her arm around my shoulders. "You need a vacation."

I sighed. She'd offered this trip about forty times in the last two weeks. "I can't take a vacation. I'm opening my marina in ten days."

"And yet, you were ready to abandon it all forever, because of a random text," she said.

I grimaced. "So I freaked out a little."

"A lot," Vinnie said. "You dove in after your cat like he was about to be murdered."

I tightened my arms around my soggy cat, who was now purring and happy to be snuggled. "I thought he was in danger."

Hattie put her hands on her hips. "As I have told you repeatedly, I'm going to visit my cousin Thelma for a couple days to celebrate her birthday. Come with me. It's a five-star island resort on the coast of Maine. You'll come back rested, refreshed, and ready to receive all texts with a clear mind."

I wanted to go so badly, because having friends was a precious new treasure, and I loved every second of it. But setting down roots in my new town was critical for me, and getting accepted by the town was more difficult than I'd expected. I had a lot riding on this grand opening, and I needed to be here working, not on vacation. "I already told you I can't. I have the grand opening—"

"If the triple X *was* from your mom, then leaving for a couple days seems like a great idea as well," Hattie interrupted.

Huh. "You're not wrong about that," I admitted slowly.

"And Lucy's coming on the trip," Hattie said. "Girl bonding. You know you love it."

Aw…Lucy was going, too? Now I really wanted to go. The three of us had become such a tight trio since I'd moved to Bass Derby.

"I think it's a good idea to go," Devlin said. "Get off the grid for a few days while we figure this out."

I looked at him, both disappointed and relieved at the idea of missing our date. "Our dinner?"

He grinned, looking pleased that I'd even remembered we had plans. "I don't know about you, but I'll still live in this town when you get back. We'll figure it out."

I bit my lip. The idea of stepping away from the marina for a couple days did sound good. I was drained, I loved

Hattie and Lucy, and a little part of me was worried that the text really had been from mom. "Is the resort cat-friendly?"

"I don't think so, but hang on." She pulled out her phone and made a call. "Beau. It's Hattie."

Beau Hammersley was a reclusive, wealthy mystery writer who claimed to hate the world, except for me, my mom, and Hattie. I suspected he liked people a lot more than he claimed, but I adored him either way.

"Mia needs to leave town for a couple days because her mom might have just sent her a cryptic text about danger. Can you come over and grab King Tut and watch him?"

I grinned. Beau was obsessed with my mom. He'd run across a documentary on the infamous Tatum Murphy when he'd been researching one of his books, and the obsession had been born.

Hattie hung up the phone. "He'll be here in a few seconds. He's around the corner. He's out boating."

My arms tightened around King Tut. "I don't want to leave King Tut behind—"

"Yo! I'm here!" Beau came flying around the corner in his boat, shouting and waving his arms. He sped up to the beach and ran his boat right onto the sand. He leapt out and came racing up. He was wearing his bejeweled sandals, denim shorts, and his tee shirt with the bloody dagger on it. His hair was ratty from the wind, and the only sign of wealth on him was the brand of his sunglasses. "Your mom's in danger?"

I almost started laughing at his delight about my mom being involved. "I don't know. Maybe."

Hattie pointed to King Tut. "Mia needs King Tut safe."

Beau eyed the cat. "Tatum might come to check on him?"

"She might," I agreed. Who knew what my mom might do? No one. Checking on my cat was as possible as anything else.

"Then he's safe with me." Beau held out his arms. "Come on, King Tut. Let's go." The reclusive mystery writer liked to put on a tough persona, but in his heart, he was a good man. If he said he'd keep King Tut safe, he would. He'd do whatever it took. After decades as a mystery writer, the man had ideas about danger, death, and murder that no one wanted to know.

King Tut gazed at Beau and didn't budge from my arms.

Beau met his steely gaze. "I have caviar."

King Tut immediately leapt out of my arms, raced down the sand, then jumped into Beau's boat. He sat down on the bow, flicked his tail, and gave us all a sullen, serious glare with his unblinking yellow eyes. Even with his black fur still dripping with water, he looked huge, menacing, and dangerous.

"Damn, girl." Hattie grinned. "If you decide not to go and deprive that cat of Beau's caviar, you will never be safe from that feline again."

"I need to channel King Tut's attitude for my next villain," Beau said. "Look at that threat. It's brilliant. Subtle. Unyielding. And yet disarming in that kitty-cat ball of soggy fluff. It's almost diabolical. I love it! He's my new muse. Get me his life jacket, and we're off."

I bit my lip. "I've never been without King Tut since I rescued him."

Hattie put her arm around my shoulder. "King Tut will be safe away from the marina, and you'll be safe too. Plus, both of you will have fun."

"I think it's the best call," Devlin said. "Give me a couple days to figure out what's going on." He looked over at me. "I'll keep an eye on the marina."

"I will, too. I know what the contractors are supposed to be doing, and I'll manage it," Vinnie said. "I'll sleep in the spare storefront. It'll cost you, but I'm worth it."

I looked at the three of them, and my heart got all mushy. These were my friends, people who cared if I died, cared if my cat was safe, and cared about my marina. I might not have had my breakthrough with the rest of the town yet, but I'd found a little niche of home, and I appreciated it with all my heart.

The truth was, I did want to go with Hattie and Lucy. I wanted to go with every fiber in my being. "How long's the trip?"

"Three days and two nights," Hattie said. "The ferry leaves in four hours, though. We need to hurry. How fast can you pack?"

I looked over at her, and suddenly, I knew she was right. They were all right. Those texts might not be from my mom, but they were the impetus I needed. I was supposed to go on this trip, and I wasn't going to miss it. "Fast."

Want more *Triple Trouble*? *Get Triple Trouble* today!

SNEAK PEEK: SECRETLY MINE

"Exquisitely beautiful!! All the feels. This is a do not pass
up book. Perfectly written :)." ~Five-star Goodreads
Review (Jann)

*She's back in town with no time for the rebel who stole her
heart long ago...but now he's playing for keeps.*

Dash Stratton had just picked up his welder when he heard
his name hollered from the front of the house.

Recognition flooded him, and he swore, spinning around. That voice sounded familiar, but there was no way Leila Sheridan would be at his house, bellowing his name.

But he'd thought he'd seen her in that car outside Wright's.

That was twice in the span of an hour.

What the hell was going on?

She, whoever it was, shouted his name again, and something prickled along his skin. He would have sworn it was Leila.

He set down the welder and strode out of his studio. He jerked his sunglasses down over his face, and headed across the lawn around the side of his house, moving with an instinctive urgency.

He practically sprinted around the side of the house, and then stopped dead, stunned.

Leila Kerrigan was in front of the house, her hands on her hips, staring right at him.

Emotions flooded him, so many emotions he couldn't sort them out. He couldn't take his gaze off her. She was a woman now, not a scrawny, scared eighteen-year-old. She was wearing shorts and sneakers, and a blue tank top, looking like she was ready for a day on the lake, like the old days.

She had curves now she hadn't had before, the curves of a woman. Her sunglasses were on top of her head, revealing those glorious blue eyes and dark lashes that he'd begun to think he'd imagined.

She sucked in her breath. "Dash."

"Fuck." He grimaced. That was all he could think of to say after all this time. "I mean, what the fuck are you doing here?"

Her eyes widened. and he swore under his breath. "Sorry. I'm just stunned to see you in my front yard. You look great." Suddenly, he realized why she was there.

She wanted a divorce. The time had come.

Fuck. This time, he meant it.

A cute little frown furrowed between her eyebrows. "You don't know why I'm here?"

Double fuck. Had her lawyer served him? Had he missed an email? "No."

"You don't know about Bea's will?"

He narrowed his eyes. Bea's will? Not a divorce? He was annoyed by the relief that shuddered through him. "What about it? I know I got the house, because she told me many times that's what she was doing." He frowned. "What did she put in there for you?" Was there something at the house that was for Leila? He hadn't seen anything with her name on it, but Bea might have hidden it well. "Do you need me to find something for you?"

Leila stared at him, then understanding dawned on her face, and she burst out laughing. "I swear to God, I'm going to kill Eppie. And Clare!"

Ah…Eppie. He knew what kind of chaos she could cause. "What did they do?" Eppie was as much trouble as Bea had been.

"Clare gave me a letter for you." She fished around in her back pocket, then held up a folded envelope. "I suspect she explains it here."

He didn't move. If it was a letter from Bea, he didn't want to read it, hear her words, feel her presence. It was too soon for him. "You explain it."

Leila waved the letter at him. "No, thanks. Here."

Swearing under his breath, Dash walked over to her to take it, but as he neared, he felt like his world was spinning. Leila Sheridan was back, and she was unfinished business. *His* unfinished business.

He took the envelope, and his fingers brushed against hers, sending a shock reverberating through his system. Yeah, the attraction was still there, but this time, she wasn't an eighteen-year-old he had to protect from a piece-of-shit stepfather.

She was a woman, and their age difference no longer

mattered like it had when she was barely eighteen and he'd been twenty-five.

When his hand touched hers, she sucked her in breath and jerked her hand back. "Letter," she mumbled.

"Letter," he agreed, as he took a step back, folded it, and put it in his pocket. "I'll read it later."

Leila's brows went up. "You need to read it now."

"I'm good. You need anything from me?"

She stared at him. "You're as stubborn and difficult as you were back then."

"Probably."

She folded her arms over her chest. "Read the letter, Dash."

"Nope." There was no chance he was reading Bea's words right now. He missed her like hell, and he wasn't in a place to read a letter she wrote to him in front of Leila. Or anyone. Or even himself. "Anything else you need?"

She stared at him. "Really?"

"Yeah. Whatever you need." This conversation felt awkward and distant, nothing like how he'd envisioned it might be all the times he'd thought about her over the years. "Want a drink? I have water and beer." And other stuff he didn't feel like mentioning.

"Water?"

"Yeah."

She put her hands on her hips. "Dash."

"Leila."

She sighed in aggravation. "Bea didn't leave you the house. She left *us* the house."

Dash stared at her. "Us?"

"Yes." She pointed back and forth between them. "You and me. Co-heirs. We have to both live in the house together for thirty consecutive nights before either of us can do anything with it. I'm moving in now."

"No." His amusement fled. Oh, wait, he hadn't been amused by anything about her sudden appearance. "It's my house. I've been living here for the last six months. She told me it was mine, repeatedly." He'd been counting on this house, and not just for himself.

"Well, it's also half mine. I need the money from selling it, and we can't sell it until we both live here together for thirty days."

Sell it? No one was selling this house. He couldn't afford to buy out Leila. He swore under his breath, then pulled out his phone and called Clare.

She answered on the first ring. "You read the letter?"

"I'm co-heirs with Leila, and we have to live in the house together for thirty consecutive nights before we can do anything with it?" It had to be wrong. It didn't make sense.

Clare sighed. "Yes, look, I'm sorry I didn't tell you, but Bea's will specifically said Leila had to be the one to tell you."

All thoughts of his attraction to Leila vanished in a surge of irritation. He ground his jaw. "So it's true?"

"Yes, it is."

He glanced at Leila, who was watching him, chewing on her lower lip. Why did she look so damned adorable chewing on her lip like that? Why did he care? He didn't have time for this. "I need this house. You know I do."

"Thirty days, Dash. You can have it in thirty days, as long as Leila agrees to give up her share."

Fuck. He couldn't afford to buy her out. "What else is in the will that you didn't tell me? There's more, isn't there? More games that Bea put in there?"

Clare cleared her throat. "It's a rather complicated will, but that's the gist of it."

He swore under his breath. "Clare—"

"Look. You could probably contest some of the provisions, but it's *Bea*," Clare said softly. "You loved her. She loved you. Don't you want to let her do this her way? Would you deprive her of that joy?"

"No." Dash rubbed his forehead and cursed again. Bea had

changed his life in many ways, standing by him when his parents disowned him. He'd spent the rest of his life giving back to her, and he couldn't stop now just because she was gone. "I'd never let her down," he admitted grudgingly.

"Bea spent a lot of time planning this," Clare said. "It's her gift to you. Not just the house, but all of it."

Dash looked at Leila. Was Leila a gift that Bea had decided to hand him? Another chance at the woman he'd let go? He ground his jaw. A year ago, cohabitating with Leila to compete for the house would have been very different than now.

Now, it didn't work for him. "Clare, she wrote the will before—"

"No, she didn't. She updated it afterwards."

That stunned Dash into silent. "She wrote it *after*?" After his whole life had changed. Rocked to its foundation. Shattered into a thousand pieces that he was still struggling to put back together. She wrote the will *after* that had happened? *What the hell, Bea?*

"Yes," Clare said. "It's your choice, Dash. You can contest it, and drag Bea's last moments of joy into question, or go with it."

He sighed. "You're very manipulative."

Clare laughed. "I know. You're welcome. Eppie and I have to confirm every night's sleepover, so you'll see a lot of us."

Roomie. Living with Leila Sheridan for thirty days. Thirty days in which to convince her to give him her half of the house. Not sell it to him. *Give* it to him.

Fuck. He didn't like needing charity from her. Bea's promise to give him the house had been his key to getting free. To have that compromised... *What the hell were you thinking, Bea?*

He didn't have a backup plan. He'd put everything into this house on the assumption he would get it.

And in those thirty days, he also had to avoid having Leila

ask for a divorce. And...he to resist the temptation that she'd been to him for a long time.

Three bedrooms.

One and a half bathrooms.

One shower.

Hell. This was going to get rough fast.

And a part of him was looking forward to every minute of it.

How hot does it get when Leila moves in? And what secret is Dash hiding? Treat yourself today to Secretly Mine, and fall in love with Dash and Leila today by clicking here!

SNEAK PEEK: BURN

"A fast-paced, heart-racing, mind-boggling, sexy
read...and I loved it!!!" ~NanaX8 (Five-star Amazon
review)

Mᴀᴄᴋ Cᴏɴɴᴏʀ ʜᴀᴅ ʙᴇᴇɴ ɪɴ Aʟᴀsᴋᴀ for less than an hour, and
he was already restless. He wanted to be back in Boston, but
when Ben Forsett asked for his help, he got it.

Always.

Every single time.

No matter what.

It had been that way since they were kids, both of them

trying to survive the streets, the drugs, and the gangs long enough to get the fuck out of the hell they'd grown up in. Ben had gone to college and law school. Mack had gone into the military and become one of the world's renowned experts on security tech, and all the shit that went with that.

Their connection had never faltered, even when life had blown up around them. Ben was the only friend Mack counted, and the only one he needed.

They always leaned on each other when the shit got real. Always. Until last month when Mack had uncovered a living hell…

"You okay?" Ben looked over at him, his brow furrowed.

Mack cleared his throat and looked out the window at the trees rushing past. So many damn trees. "Yeah. Fine."

"What happened last month?"

Mack shot a sharp glance at Ben. "Nothing."

"Bullshit. Something fucked you up. What was it?"

For a split second, Mack was tempted to tell Ben the truth, to rip the darkness out of him and throw it onto his friend.

But just as quickly, he shoved it back down inside him, deep and hard, where it couldn't see the light of day.

"Nothing." He wasn't going there. He just fucking wasn't. He hadn't told Ben about it then, and he wasn't going to tell him now.

Darkness settled in him, and he growled as he dragged his thoughts away from the nightmare that had jerked him awake every single night for the last month. "How about you?" Ben had been through hellacious year.

Ben hesitated, and Mack saw the moment that he decided not to push Mack for more answers. "Better. Mari helps. A lot."

Mack nodded. "Good." He was glad Ben had found someone who fit him. "I can't believe you proposed to her."

Ben smiled, a legit grin that lit up his face. "She changed my world, bro. She's a gift."

A sliver of envy flickered through Mack at the happiness on his friend's face. He'd never seen him like that before. It hadn't even occurred to him that either of them would ever feel that, that it could be a part of their lives. "Damn, man," he said softly. "I'm almost jealous of that stupid grin."

Ben's smile faded into seriousness. "I'm staying in Alaska. I've found peace here."

"Not coming back to Boston?" Mack felt darkness settle in him again. He and Ben had both been in Boston for the last few years, and it had settled him to have Ben around again. Having him move to Alaska? *Shit.* But he grinned at his friend anyway. "Good for you." He meant it, too.

Ben cocked an eyebrow at him. "You might like it here, too. It's an amazing place."

Mack snorted and jerked his thumb at mountains in the distance. "Where are my skyscrapers? No fucking way."

"That's what I thought, too. Things change."

"Not for me." Mack shifted, suddenly restless to get back to topics he felt comfortable with.

They'd spent the first part of the drive from the airport going over the serial killer he'd helped Ben track a few weeks ago, and now it was time to focus on the present.

"Talk to me," he said. "What do you need me for?" He knew it must be bad for Ben to ask him to fly to Alaska for it. The fact Ben had refused to give any details over the phone about why he needed him had jacked up his adrenaline even more.

Ben glanced over at him as his truck bounced over the rutted dirt road. "Mari's friend. Charlotte."

Charlotte. Mack liked the name. He wasn't sure why. It was soft and strong at the same time. He knew nothing about soft, and he didn't particularly want to, but her name seemed to settle in him whenever he heard it.

"The one who got kidnapped." He'd tracked her phone for Ben to help find her. "She doing okay?"

Ben inclined his head. "Sort of."

Mack narrowed his eyes, studying Ben. "You brought me here for her?"

At Ben's nod, Mack settled into the familiarity of business mode. "What's she into?" He unzipped his backpack and pulled out his computer. It booted up instantly, and he created a file with her name. "Her last name is Murphy, right?"

"Yep." Ben rattled off her address, and Mack entered it into the computer.

"What else?"

"That's it."

Mack looked up. "What do you mean, that's it? What's going on with her?"

"I don't know." Ben took a right, the truck lurching over a big rut in the dirt. "It's something though. Something from her past."

Mack frowned. "A person? A man? Something someone else did? Something she did?" The last question stopped him hard. He knew all about someone who had done something bad, something that came back to haunt him. He was not getting involved with someone who had done bad shit. Not again. He cast a suspicious look at Ben. "How well do you know her?"

"Not well, but she's good. She's been Mari's friend since the day she arrived in town."

Not well. Mack closed the lid to his computer. "Look. I owe you a thousand times over, but I'm not feeling this one."

"You will." Ben slowed the truck. "I arranged for you to stay at her place with her."

"No." Mack put his computer away and zipped up his backpack. "Absolutely not. I live alone. I hate people, except for you. And even you I don't want in my space."

At that moment, Ben's phone rang. He hit the speaker button. "Hey, sweetheart."

212

Sweetheart? Mack frowned at his friend as a woman's voice filled the car.

"Hey, babe. We have a problem," she said. "Charlotte says Mack can't stay with her, and she's leaving town. She's inside packing right now."

Mack couldn't help but grin. He liked the fact that Charlotte was refusing to be railroaded by Ben. The woman had backbone. "See? It's been decided."

"Mack? Is that Mack?" The warmth in Mari's voice surprised him. "I'm so glad you're here. Ben's told me so much about you. Charlotte needs you."

Her words ripped the smile off his face. "Charlotte appears to disagree with you both." He tried to sound civil, but he knew he wasn't particularly good at it.

"She freaked out when we got here, Ben," Mari said, ignoring Mack so completely that he got a little more respect for her. "I thought she was going to leap out of her skin when I knocked on her window. She was scanning the woods like she knew someone was watching her. It freaked me out, too."

Her words piqued Mack's interest, despite his reluctance. A woman in danger was a dangerous trigger for him right now, even more than usual. "You think it was nerves from the attack?"

"No." Her convocation was absolute. "It definitely had to do with someone else. Whoever it was that she said would be coming back for her."

"Coming back?" Mack leaned forward, listening more intently. "When did she say that?"

"At the hospital, when she found out that the story had been in the papers and on the Internet. She said he'd see it, and he'd come back. She was so freaked when she got home."

Ben swore under his breath and shot a scowl at Mack, as if it were his fault.

"Joseph found me," Mari said, her voice cracking slightly.

"There's nowhere to hide if someone wants to find her. We all know that."

Mack did know that. He was one of the ones who could find anyone. And he'd completely fucked it up a month ago.

"We'll talk to her when we get there." Ben's voice was gentle, gentler than Mack had ever heard him use. "You doing okay, Mari?"

"Yeah. She kind of wigged me out, but Haas is here, so I'm okay."

"Haas Carter?" Mack repeated the name, fighting the temptation to open his computer back up and add it to Charlotte's file. Ben had such praise for the old-timer Alaskan that Mack was actually interested in meeting him.

"Yes, he's here—" Mari paused. "Charlotte's coming out the door now with a bag. Haas says he won't shoot her to make her stay. How far away are you?"

"We're here."

As Ben spoke, the truck rounded a bend, and a well-worn log cabin came into view. A second building had part of the frame up, a couple trucks were in the driveway, and an old man and a woman were next to the bigger one.

But what caught Mack's attention was the woman jogging down her front steps with a duffel bag that was twice as big as she was. On her heels was a gorgeous German shepherd, glued to her side as if it were trained to perfection.

But it wasn't the dog that riveted his attention.

It was the woman. Charlotte.

It wasn't the gorgeous dark waves of her hair. Or the rigid set of her shoulders that told him of a raw, inner strength. Or the way her jeans hugged her hips like they were made for her.

It was the way she stared at the woods, terror etched over every line of her body as she came to a sudden stop.

She spoke to the dog, who took off at a sprint, nose to the ground as he bolted into the trees.

Mack was peripherally aware that Ben and the two folks in the driveway had paused to watch the dog.

He didn't.

He watched Charlotte.

She remained still, but she wasn't watching the dog either. She was carefully scanning her property, her gaze focused and methodical, as if she knew exactly what she was looking for while she waited for the dog to finish.

After her survey, he saw her shoulders loosen infinitesi-mally. She then raised her gaze to the dog, who was trotting back, his body at ease, and his tail waving peacefully.

She relaxed more, and held out her hand to the dog, who ground his head affectionately into her palm as she spoke softly to him.

The brief moment had told Mack much.

She was strong.

She was smart.

She was good to her dog.

And whoever was hunting her had been doing it for long enough that she'd developed a defense system, one that she no longer believed could keep her safe.

He swore under his breath as Ben pulled up beside an old, battered pickup truck that he assumed belonged to Haas.

Charlotte looked up and saw Ben's truck. As soon as she realized he was there, for a split second, she relaxed, a full and complete release that made her face soften.

Mack knew it was because Ben's appearance made her feel safe, and for that split second, she leaned into it, grasping for a respite from being constantly on edge. He liked that she trusted Ben. It showed she had good sense. Ben was the only person he trusted, so he appreciated that Charlotte could see that about him as well.

Then her gaze went to the passenger seat, and she realized Mack was with him.

Her jaw immediately jutted out. She pulled her shoulders

back. And she set her hands on her hips. A fighting stance that made him grin.

"She's ready to kick you out before you even move in," Ben said, resting his forearms on the steering wheel.

"I see that."

Ben cocked an eyebrow at him. "What are you going to do about it?"

Mack leaned forward, watching Charlotte. She was too far away to see clearly, and he knew she couldn't see him well behind the windshield. "She believes she'll be attacked in her own home," he observed.

"I agree." Ben drummed his fingers on the dash. "What if you walk away, and that happens to her?"

Mack was unable to take his gaze off her as she stared him down. She was attitude and sass, even when she was scared shitless. He respected that. Which made Ben's question jab right into his gut and twist its blade. *What if he walked away, and she was killed?* "Really? That's the line you're throwing my way to get me to stay?"

"Yep." Ben cocked an eyebrow. "Did it work?"

Mack sighed and picked up his backpack. "Fuck you, Forsett." He grabbed the door handle and stepped out of the truck.

Ben leaned across the seat, grinning at him. "So, that's a yes? It worked?"

Mack's only answer was to slam the door in his friend's face, but he was grinning as he heard Ben's laughter.

Yeah, it had worked.

Charlotte Murphy was officially his next case.

Like it? Get it now!

A QUICK FAVOR

Did you enjoy Bella and Falcon's story?

People are often hesitant to try new books or new authors. A few reviews can encourage them to make that leap and give it a try. If you enjoyed *A Rogue Cowboy's Kiss* and think others will as well, please consider taking a moment and writing one or two sentences on the etailer and/or Goodreads *to* help this story find the readers who would enjoy it. Even the short reviews really make an impact!

Thank you a million times for reading my books! I love writing for you and sharing the journeys of these beautiful characters with you. I hope you find inspiration from their stories in your own life!

Love,
Stephanie

STEPHANIE ROWE BOOKS

STEPHANIE ROWE BOOKS

THE HART RANCH BILLIONAIRES SERIES
(CONTEMPORARY WESTERN ROMANCE)
A Rogue Cowboy's Second Chance
A Rogue Cowboy's Christmas Surprise
A Rogue Cowboy Finds Love
A Rogue Cowboy's Heart
A Rogue Cowboy's Kiss

WYOMING REBELS SERIES
(CONTEMPORARY WESTERN ROMANCE)
A Real Cowboy Never Says No
A Real Cowboy Knows How to Kiss
A Real Cowboy Rides a Motorcycle
A Real Cowboy Never Walks Away
A Real Cowboy Loves Forever
A Real Cowboy for Christmas
A Real Cowboy Always Trusts His Heart
A Real Cowboy Always Protects
A Real Cowboy for the Holidays
A Real Cowboy Always Comes Home
SERIES COMPLETE

LINKED TO THE HART RANCH BILLIONAIRES SERIES
(CONTEMPORARY WESTERN ROMANCE)
Her Rebel Cowboy

BIRCH CROSSING SERIES
(SMALL-TOWN CONTEMPORARY ROMANCE)
Unexpectedly Mine
Accidentally Mine
Unintentionally Mine
Irresistibly Mine
Secretly Mine

ORDER OF THE BLADE SERIES
(PARANORMAL ROMANCE)
Darkness Awakened
Darkness Seduced
Darkness Surrendered
Forever in Darkness
Darkness Reborn
Darkness Arisen
Darkness Unleashed
Inferno of Darkness
Darkness Possessed
Shadows of Darkness
Hunt the Darkness
Darkness Awakened: Reimagined

ROMANTIC SUSPENSE

ALASKA HEAT SERIES
(ROMANTIC SUSPENSE)
Ice
Chill
Ghost
Burn
Hunt (novella)

BOXED SETS

Order of the Blade (Books 1-4)
Protectors of the Heart (A Six-Book First-in-Series Collection)
Wyoming Rebels Boxed Set (Books 1-3)

For a complete list of Stephanie's books, go to www. stephanierowe.com.

ABOUT THE AUTHOR

New York Times and *USA Today* bestselling author Stephanie Rowe is the author of more than sixty published novels. Notably, she is a Vivian® Award nominee, a RITA® Award winner and a five-time nominee, and a Golden Heart® Award winner and two-time nominee. As the author of more than sixty novels, Stephanie loves strong, sexy protective book boyfriends and the sassy, smart heroines who win their hearts. Humor, melt-worthy romance, and heat for the win! She has written for Grand Central Publishing, Harlequin, HarperCollins, Sourcebooks, and Dorchester Publishing.

She loves her puppies, tennis, and trying to live her best,

truest life. Stephanie believes strongly in the power of women, and she hopes that in every book, she gives every reader a little hope, or smile, or simply a heart-warming escape into a world that brings her joy. For info on Stephanie's newest releases, join her newsletter today!

www.stephanierowe.com

Made in the USA
Monee, IL
25 January 2025

10933385R00142